nine, ten:

A SEPTEMBER 11 STORY

Also by Nora Raleigh Baskin

The Truth About My Bat Mitzvah
Anything But Typical
The Summer Before Boys
Runt
Ruby on the Outside

nine, ten:

A SEPTEMBER 11 STORY

Nora Raleigh Baskin

Atheneum Books for Young Readers
New York London Toronto Sydney New Delhi

ATHENEUM BOOKS FOR YOUNG READERS | An imprint of Simon & Schuster Children's Publishing Division | 1230 Avenue of the Americas, New York, New York 10020 | This book is a work of fiction. Any references to historical events, real people, or real places are used fictitiously. Other names, characters, places, and events are products of the author's imagination, and any resemblance to actual events or places or persons, living or dead, is entirely coincidental. | For information about special discounts for bulk purchases, please contact Simon & Schuster Special Sales at 1-866-506-1949 or business@simonandschuster.com. | The Simon & Schuster Speakers Bureau can bring authors to your live event. For more information or to book an event, contact the Simon & Schuster Speakers Bureau at 1-866-248-3049 or visit our website at www.simonspeakers.com. | Also available in an Atheneum Books for Young Readers hardcover edition | Interior design by Mike Rosamilia | The text for this book was set in Adobe Caslon Pro. | Manufactured in the United States of America | 0519 OFF | First Atheneum Books for Young Readers paperback edition May 2017 | 10 9 8 7 | The Library of Congress has cataloged the hardcover edition as follows: | Baskin, Nora Raleigh. | Nine, ten : a September 11 story / Nora Raleigh Baskin. — First edition. | pages cm | Summary: Relates how the lives of four children living in different parts of the country intersect and are affected by the events of September 11, 2001. | ISBN 978-1-4424-8506-8 (hc) | ISBN 978-1-4424-8507-5 (pbk) | ISBN 978-1-4424-8508-2 (eBook) 1. September 11 Terrorist Attacks, 2001—Juvenile fiction. [1. September 11 Terrorist Attacks, 2001—Fiction.] I. Title. | PZ7.B29233Ni 2016 | [Fic]—dc22 2015011934

For the children, our future

Everyone will mention the same thing, and if they don't, when you ask them, they will remember. It was a perfect day.

More than eight million people lived in New York City that year, so of course, not everyone's day started perfectly. There was excitement and pain, anxiety and boredom, love and loneliness, anger and joy. But everyone who looked up that morning must have marveled, whether noting it out loud or not: *What a perfect day*.

The sky was robin's-egg blue. There were one or two fluffy, almost decorative clouds. It was late-summer warm, so the air was still and clear, not the least bit humid. Warm the exact way you would set the temperature of the earth, if you could. Clear, with just enough breeze so you knew you were outside, breathing fresh air. People would remember that day with all sorts of adjectives: serene, lovely, cheerful, invigorating, peaceful, quiet, astounding, crystalline, blue.

Perfect.

Until 8:46 a.m., when the first plane struck the North Tower of the World Trade Center and nothing would ever be the same again.

But that has not happened yet.

9/9

September 9, 2001
7:46 a.m. CDT
O'Hare International Airport

It was September 9, 2001, raining in that Chicago slow-drizzle sort of way. Outside the windows of O'Hare International Airport, the sky was painted a particular shade of gray and leaving droplets of water on the large glass windows that looked out onto the airstrip.

Sergio and another boy from New York were at the gate, early for their flight home. Their university escort was sitting, eyes closed, listening to her Discman, waiting for the boys to board so she could go home.

What was the other boy's name? Sergio couldn't remember. *L*-something? Or *M*-something? For two days Sergio had recognized him as, simply, the white boy with the red hair.

"Let's go see what's in the candy shop."

The redheaded boy pointed to the newsstand, which was filled with everything anyone could possibly think of needing before getting onto a plane: newspapers, magazines, headrests, paperback novels, earphones, small suitcases, cold drinks, and lots of candy.

Sergio glanced over at the escort, who didn't look up. She didn't even open her eyes.

"Okay," Sergio said. He took one more glance around to make sure they could find their way back to their gate. Everything in the airport appeared the same, every corner, every window, every set of plastic seats, every gate. It would be easy to get lost. Sergio made sure he would not. Then he checked the information on the board again.

Flight 563, JFK.

On time, gate 10.

His grandmother would be getting up right about now. It was Sunday. Her one day to sleep in. But she was probably up already, making coffee, knowing Sergio would be home in a few hours.

Sergio didn't realize how homesick he was, he *had* been, the whole time, until just then, when he started thinking about his grandmother. It was the first time he had ever been away from home. And he'd only agreed to go at all because his grandma was so proud of him.

Five kids from New York State had been chosen to be honored at this ceremony at the University of Chicago, all based on one math test they had taken at the end of last year. And for that Sergio had been flown to Chicago, put up in a hotel, and given three meals a day, and when they had called his name—his full name, Sergio Kinkaid Williams—he had walked across the gigantic stage of the Court Theatre and received his plaque, which was now weighing down his carry-on bag as he perused the newsstand.

Kinkaid was his father's last name. Of his father, that was pretty much all he *wanted* to know.

"You getting anything to eat?" the redheaded boy asked when they got into the checkout line.

Sergio slipped his hand into his jeans pocket to feel the twenty-dollar bill his grandmother had given him three days ago. He didn't want to break it if he didn't have to.

"Don't they give us lunch or breakfast or something on the plane?"

"Yeah, but they won't give us Kit Kat bars." The boy with the red hair put two candy bars on the counter.

Sergio shook his head. "Nah, I'm good."

They finished checking out, and the boy handed Sergio one of the Kit Kats. "I hate to eat alone," he said.

"Thanks." Sergio took the candy. He wasn't expecting that. It was nice.

The redheaded boy began to unwrap his candy, then stopped. He appeared to be more interested in something across the store. "That is so weird, isn't it?" he said. He pointed. "What's she got on her head?"

Sergio tried to figure out what the boy was talking about, but didn't see anything. "What's weird? Who?"

"Her." The boy gestured across the news shop, to a girl with her back toward them, facing a full wall of magazines.

She was wearing regular clothes, jeans and a sweater, but her head was wrapped in a shawl, a thin brown veil. Sergio knew what that meant. She was Muslim. There were a lot of Muslim girls in his neighborhood and in his school, but this kid had probably never seen anyone dressed like that. He was from way upstate New York somewhere.

At that moment the girl turned toward them as if she had heard them talking. Her head scarf completely covered her head and neck, all the way down to her shoulders. Like a child's drawing, her pale face was floating in a sea of brown fabric. Her lips pressed together. Her brow furrowed. Her eyes were blue, like the Mediterranean Sea.

"Hey, man. Let's go," Sergio said.

It was so not cool to stare.

Naheed was used to it. Being looked at. She was used to people asking if she was wearing a costume. Or saying:

"I didn't know you were Arab."

"Can you belly dance?"

"Do you believe in God?"

"Do you really not eat for a month?"

She wasn't Arab. She was Middle Eastern. Well, she was American, born twelve years ago in Columbus, Ohio, and she had never lived anywhere else. She had never once been to Iran, where her Persian mother and father had grown up. She couldn't belly dance either.

But she was used to people staring as soon as she left her house, her neighborhood, her school, her friends, and was out in public, as she was here in O'Hare Airport, waiting for her uncle and aunt to arrive.

Their flight hadn't come in yet. Naheed's family could have just waited outside for Uncle Iman and Aunt Judith to go through security and baggage, but her dad wanted to be right at the gate when his brother got off the plane, so they had gotten to the airport early. Really early. They had already had snacks, gone to the bathroom, and wandered through all the gift shops, and Uncle Iman's plane was still not here.

"Why don't you get yourself a magazine?" Naheed's father offered. "One I would approve of," he quickly added.

Naheed gazed at the display wall. There were hundreds of magazines, all with exciting, colorful covers, pretty girls, beautiful clothing, and lots of bare skin. But there wasn't one magazine on this wall her father would let her buy. The girls with their hair blowing freely all around their heads like someone had a fan right in their faces, their bare arms showing even though they were advertising winter fashions; Naheed knew it was immodest.

"A girl does not need to flaunt her beauty to the world," her mother had told her many times. "Real beauty is inside, and the right boy will see that."

Naheed decided she didn't need anything after all. She turned to head back to her family. Only now there were people everywhere, filling the news shop, heading in all directions, strolling, rushing, dragging children and bags, but nowhere did she see her mother's or father's or little sister's familiar face.

Her father had been standing right there a minute ago. Hadn't he?

Naheed looked straight ahead in the direction she had just come from. Or was it that way? Or there? It all looked the same. There were faces everywhere, but no one she knew.

Her heart started to pump more quickly, and she felt the heat filling up her body. A tiny band of sweat formed instantly across her forehead. How would she ever find them?

She could feel tears springing into the corners of her eyes.

There were people all around her. Too many people. Too many faces. She didn't want to start crying, but it was about to happen anyway. She kept walking, looking down at the ground, hoping her feet would keep working even if her brain wasn't. In this way she banged directly into something solid, unmoving, and talking.

"Hey, watch where you're going."

Naheed looked up. It was so weird—for a second it seemed that a girl from one of those magazines had actually stepped out and was here, right in front of her.

Light brown hair, long and straight, carefully pulled away from her face and delicate neck. She had perfect skin, and a perfect outfit: white T-shirt with some kind of logo, tucked into her belted jeans.

"Oh no, now look what happened," the girl said.

The impact of two bodies had sent the girl's bag spilling onto the floor. ChapStick. A water bottle, a Walkman, and a plastic change purse, unfortunately not quite tightly closed.

"I'm sorry. I didn't mean to. . . ." Now surely Naheed was going to cry. She began to bend down next to the girl to help her, when she saw, across the way, her little sister, Nouri, waving her arms.

"Here! Here," Nouri was saying.

Naheed felt a wash of comfort pour over her. Her mind cleared. Her heart slowed with relief, then sped back up with joy.

She hadn't lost them.

There was her family, standing by the far window. The plane had arrived. Even Uncle Iman and Aunt Judith were a welcome sight.

Naheed stopped trying to collect the girl's things. She stood up.

"Oh, never mind," the girl said, wisps of her hair now loose and falling into her eyes as she gathered her things from the floor. "I got it."

"Sorry. I mean thanks," Naheed called back. "I mean sorry." But her voice was absorbed into the airport terminal din.

* * *

Aimee grabbed for the loose coin that was standing upright and rolling across the floor, but it got away. She didn't feel like chasing it. She let her mind glaze over, watching the nickel or dime or quarter or whatever it was turn like a wheel, to the left, to the right, and left again, before it finally toppled over and a man's thick black shoe stepped right on it, then he went on his way without noticing.

"Aimee, what are you doing on the floor?" her mother asked. "You know I'm in a rush."

Aimee knew that. Her mother needed to hurry to catch her flight. Aimee and her dad were going to Los Angeles, but her mom, at the last minute, had to go to New York for a meeting. Her new job meant that "last minute" happened a lot. It meant nights and sometimes even weekends.

And sometimes Aimee just wished her mom's new job had never happened.

"Do you *have* to go?" Aimee could hear herself whining, but she couldn't help it. She was starting seventh grade tomorrow in a new school, in a new town, and, to make matters worse, a week later than everyone else because of the bat mitzvah.

She might still have been whining about *that*, except

her cousin's bat mitzvah had been so much fun. Aimee's family had already sold their house, so for the weekend of the bat mitzvah they got to stay in the Drake Hotel. Aimee could have stayed down the hall, with her other out-of-town cousins, all girls about her age, but she chose to stay with her parents, like she used to when she was little and they would go away on vacation. If there were two queen-size beds in the room, she would make her parents sleep separately, so that one night she could sleep with one and the next night the other. Her favorite vacation was when they went to the Magic Kingdom in Orlando, and there was only one king bed. She slept right in the middle, with her mother and father on either side of her.

This time, at the Drake Hotel, they ordered a roll-away brought to the room, but it felt nearly as good. After the bat mitzvah party, when they went back to their room, all the decorative pillows had been taken off the king bed, and the covers were turned down into a perfect triangle. Even her little rollaway had been folded down neatly, set up for her just to climb right in and go to sleep. There were two tiny wrapped chocolates on all of their pillows.

Aimee knew she was too old to want to be sleeping in the same room with her parents, but she couldn't help it. She hated it when her mother was about to leave on a business trip.

But now as her mother kissed her good-bye and left, Aimee didn't say anything. She didn't want to start crying. She waved as she watched her mother getting farther and farther away.

There was still time. She could run after her mother and stop her from leaving. In her mind Aimee played out the scene. She would catch up in a few seconds, before her mother could turn around at the sound of Aimee's sneakers. Aimee would wrap her arms around her mother's waist and hold tight, really tight. They would stay that way for a few moments, hugging, not having to say anything because there would be nothing to say.

I love you, Mamaleh.

I love you, too, Aimeleh.

And then her mother wouldn't get on the plane. She'd stay home with Aimee and they would bake cookies.

Aimee could still make it.

Now.

If she ran fast.

She even felt the energy tingle in her toes.

But she didn't run, and then, *poof*, the moment was gone, and now there was a stranger, a woman with two little girls hiding behind their mother's legs, talking to Aimee's dad. And there was a boy standing beside the mom, looking embarrassed but protective.

"Excuse me," the mother was saying.

"Yes?" Aimee's father answered.

"I'm sorry, but do you have the time?"

"Of course."

Aimee's dad looked at his watch and told her the time. At the same time he reached over and gave Aimee a squeeze. He knew she needed it. The woman said, "Thank you," and she and her three kids headed off somewhere in a big hurry. When Aimee looked back down the corridor, her mother was gone.

Maybe it was the way the dad put his arm around the girl when he was looking at his watch. Or maybe it was how the girl kind of looked like Claire, a little bit. They had the same color hair, and Claire wore hers that way too. She was about the same height. But maybe it was just the way the dad was being so attentive to his kid that Will noticed.

And he felt a tiny, sharp pain in his throat.

"You didn't need to bother that man," Will said when they had walked past. "There's the time, Mom. Right up there on the board." He pointed.

"I know, I know, but I wanted to double-check," his mother said. "Just to make sure."

Will and his two sisters, Rooney and Callie, followed their mother through the airport. He wished his mother didn't get so nervous. He really wished she didn't ask strangers for help all the time. And that had nothing to do with his dad dying or the way he got killed. Died or killed, Will wasn't sure, because he still didn't have the right words to explain his father's death. To make sense of any of it. To even think about it.

No, his mom had *always* been like that, talking to anyone, thinking that the universe took care of you, as if all you had to do was ask nicely. She acted as if she really believed people in this world cared about other people and would actually stick their neck out, just because *she* did that for other people. Because that was the right thing to do.

Or because that's how their dad had always done things.

"Come on, kids." Will's mother was doing her speed-walking thing through the terminal. "We have to hurry."

This trip to Florida hadn't been a such a good idea all around. But what could they do? It had been given to them, everything—including tickets to Disney World—all paid for; a gift of healing from the town of

Shanksville. A bunch of his parents' friends had decided the family needed to get away on the anniversary, if you could call it that.

The whole town, practically, had raised the money, quietly and not so quietly, through bake sales and donations and gifts, and so when they presented the trip to Will's mom, what could she say? No?

No, thank you.

My family and I don't want to have fun anymore.

The lines at Disney World had been so long, the wait sometimes more than an hour, and it had been hot. Callie fell asleep, and their mother ended up carrying her through most of the Magic Kingdom. She looked like a limp doll, a sweaty limp doll. Rooney cried after each ride because she wanted to go again, but you couldn't do that.

Life doesn't work that way, not even in the Magic Kingdom.

The trip began to feel like a burden. It was a chore to be happy, even though sometimes, in spite of themselves, they *were* happy. Like when Callie jumped into the pool and made it all the way to the other side by herself. Or when the French waitress at Epcot brought them a dessert meant for another table but told them they could keep it anyway. They took four spoons and dug in, not having any idea what it was.

"Dad would have loved this," Rooney said, scraping the last of the rich, creamy pudding from the bowl with her finger.

"Daddy loved cinnamon," their mother added.

And they all got quiet again.

By the end of the long weekend they all were exhausted.

They were fifty-eight minutes early for their connecting flight home. Orlando to Chicago. Now Chicago to Pittsburgh. The waiting area was practically empty. Will's sisters both laid their heads down on their mother's lap.

Will pulled a watch out of his pocket. It wasn't one of those new cool watches that told the temperature and what time it was all over the world. It was just a plain Timex on an old, really worn yellow-and-blue-striped fabric band, but it had been his dad's watch. The only thing Will had specifically asked for.

When Will was little, his dad used to let him wind it up, pulling out the tiny stem and turning the metal knob, careful never to overwind. Mindful, as well, never to let it stop completely. Will held the watch in his hand and looked down at the white face, the black roman numerals, and the skinny second hand ticking forward in a steady, jerking beat.

It was 10:03 exactly.

9/10

September 10, 2001
6:45 a.m. EDT
Shanksville, Pennsylvania

Will's sisters were already in their usual spots at the kitchen table, arguing over the positioning of a cereal box for the best viewing, when he made his way down for breakfast.

"Coffee?" His mother handed him a mug.

"Thanks," Will said. He turned to Rooney and Callie. "What's so important about the Fruity Pebbles?"

"There's a game on the back," Rooney whined.

"Yeah, and it's my turn." Callie shifted the box in her direction.

Rooney yanked it back.

"Okay, that's enough." Will stepped over and lifted the box off the table. "Now no one gets to play."

The girls didn't seem to mind. They both quieted and

returned to slurping down their bowls of pastel-colored leftover milk.

"Thanks, Will." His mother wanted to say more, Will could tell, but she knew better than to heap compliments on him that felt like obligations. He was the quiet type, just as his dad had been. Too much conversation had made them both—now just Will—uncomfortable.

Maybe his mother wanted to tell Will how great he had been ever since you-know-when. Maybe she was going to thank him for picking up the slack, helping out with the house and the girls. He had even tried to help her with the mountain of paperwork and red tape that had been dumped on them in order to get survivor benefits from the trucking company.

Will had certainly stepped up, everyone said so. He heard it all the time. He was the best son any mother could ever hope to have in a situation like this—a young father dying, so randomly, so violently, leaving behind a wife and three children.

But that was the thing. He'd left them. Because the truth was that Will's father should never have died. It didn't have to happen. All his father had had to do was call in the accident on his CB. And if he'd really wanted to do something, if he'd really *had* to do something, he could have sat in his truck and waited for help to arrive.

How many times had he himself warned Will?

Nothing good happens on the road after midnight.

There are too many bad drivers out there.

Will's dad was not one of them. In his eighteen years of long-distance hauling he had never gotten a serious infraction. Never even gotten a speeding ticket. Maybe that made this all the more ironic; it certainly seemed more unfair. It was unfair and it was wrong.

Will's father would often be on the road for days, sometimes weeks. And so when he came home, it always felt like a vacation for all of them, even if Will and the girls had school and their mom still went to work. It changed the atmosphere in the house to something festive. It was a holiday just to have him home.

It didn't hurt that their dad always brought presents from wherever he had been. California. Nevada. New Jersey. South Carolina. Little things; maybe something from a truck stop or a diner or a Holiday Inn. A pack of cards for one of the girls. A kachina doll for the other. A Matchbox car for Will. A plastic ring that came inside a plastic egg for their mom, and she would wear it all day. Sometimes just a folded map, or a paper menu from a restaurant with an interesting history. Or a pack of gum.

But he always had something for each one of them, every time.

Until he didn't come home at all.

The state troopers showed up at their door before any of them had a chance to wonder where he was, or why he hadn't called in before he reached his next checkpoint. No one was missing him. None of them knew enough to wonder why the police were knocking.

"Mrs. Rittenhouse?" The short one took off his hat.

Looking back, Will thought that should have been a warning sign. The tall one had his eyes down until he had to speak. "Mrs. Frank Rittenhouse?" he asked.

And after that it was pretty much a blur, bits and pieces of information, and images no one would want taking up residence in one's brain.

Apparently, Will's dad had been on his way home after being on the road for two and a half weeks, making the trip home from Denver, when he saw a car not quite pulled over on the side of the interstate and the driver, a man clearly in distress, slumped over the steering wheel. Smoke was coming from under the hood. Most likely, he had hit a deer.

Never pull over on the side of the interstate.

It's dangerous.

Always try to find a rest stop, an exit, or a bypass road.

"Your husband was trying to help," the tall one said, but of course it was all speculation. That's what those state troopers did, put together accident scenes based on the physical evidence. Fur and blood in the grille of the first car. Tire tracks, amount and location of damage to both cars.

In this case they figured Will's dad had seen a fellow motorist in trouble, stopped his rig a few feet ahead of the disabled car, walked over, and been about to open the driver's door to see what was wrong when another car came racing down the highway.

"Your dad was a hero," the state trooper went on, but Will could tell he didn't mean it.

A hero?

It was a stupid thing his father had done. Getting out of his truck, standing on the side of the interstate that way. He had warned his own family against doing that hundreds of times. If they were out in their station wagon and he saw someone changing a tire by the side of the road, he would roll down his window.

"Don't do that, mister. It's dangerous. Call a tow."

The state troopers went on to describe, briefly, how the oncoming car hit the disabled vehicle and sent it into the side of the rocky embankment with Will's dad pinned between them. Listening, Will and his mom remained silent. The girls were upstairs. It had been over quickly, the troopers were certain.

He was a hero. They repeated that.

And then Will's mother asked the strangest question. "What happened to the man in the car?"

"The one that hit them, ma'am?"

"No," she said. "The man my husband was trying to help?"

Both troopers seemed to breathe in simultaneously, like they had a long day ahead of them, a long unpleasant day. They could have more houses to visit, more news to deliver. Or maybe this was their only assignment for the whole day, and it was already too much.

Finally the short one spoke. "He died, ma'am. They both died."

So it was all for nothing.

"You didn't eat anything," Will's mom was saying.

It would upset her more if he didn't eat. She'd feel like a bad mother. She needed to feel useful. It had been a full year since they lost their dad, about the time people start to get past their grief, but no one, it seemed, had bothered to tell that to Will's family.

"I'll take an English muffin if you'll make one. I gotta go back up and get my sneakers," Will said.

His mother burst into action, fussing like a frantic chicken. She was almost more at ease when she was rushing about nervously. When Will came back down-stairs, she was standing with his breakfast wrapped in foil.

"You're so good to me," she said.

So he hadn't fooled anyone pretending to be hungry. His mother kissed him on the cheek and then pushed him toward the front door. There was an invisible wall between the world out there, where his father's death *wasn't* ever-present, and the world in here, where it *always* was. Will felt it blocking him, tugging at him every time he had to leave the house.

Then, out the window, Will could see the flash of school-bus yellow through the trees, and his heart jumped a tiny beat faster. His feet unstuck. He stepped outside.

Claire would be on the bus.

September 10, 2001
10:14 a.m. PDT
Los Angeles, California

Aimee had been too young to see the movie *Clueless* when it first came out in theaters, but she had seen it several times since then, and she owned the video tape. It was one of her favorites, but it had never entered her mind that one day she'd be living in Los Angeles and going to a school that looked just like the one Cher Horowitz went to.

But it did. It looked just like that school. Right down to the sunshine and the sea of blond hair.

"Why do we have lunch at ten o'clock in the morning?" a voice next to Aimee was complaining.

Aimee turned to see who was talking. It was a girl about her age, which made sense, since this was the seventh-grade lunch period. But Aimee wasn't hungry, and she hadn't felt like negotiating the line, or trying to figure out how to buy lunch and where to sit or with whom. And apparently no one else wanted to eat either, since it looked like most everyone else was here in front of the middle school, spread out over the lawn and steps, instead of in the cafeteria.

The answer came. "Because *some* grade has to get early lunch period."

"It's not that I want to eat their horrible lunch anyway, but this is ridiculous. Don't you have any sunscreen in your bag?"

The voices were coming from two girls who were sitting on the same stone wall Aimee had found. It was under the shade of a large tree with droopy branches covered in beautiful purple flowers that gave off the most amazing scent, like real perfume. They definitely didn't have trees like *this* at Aimee's school in Chicago.

Or girls like that.

They looked like miniature grown-ups, in perfect clothing, with perfect haircuts, perfect skin.

Aimee looked down at the jeans, flouncy white blouse, and brand-new sneakers that had seemed just fine just this morning but suddenly looked ridiculous. She looked like a baby. Oh jeez, what had she been thinking?

If her mother had been home, they would have laid

out her outfit the night before. They might even have gone shopping for something special. But as it was, most of her stuff was still packed in boxes, and her mother's trip to New York hadn't been expected when they made plans to stay an extra week for the bat mitzvah.

Aimee had had to leave her school, her house, her room, and all her friends, including her best friend, Lauren, who had sobbed and cried, and had made Aimee a special memory book, which she'd held out in one hand, wiping her nose with the other.

"I'm not moving to outer space," Aimee had said, but she could feel a flood of tears behind her own eyes, and now, looking out at her new school, she wasn't sure she *hadn't* landed on the moon.

"Who are *you*?" It was one of the girls sitting on the wall beside Aimee. The one who wanted the sunscreen.

"Me?" Aimee pointed to herself.

"No, the girl behind you."

And Aimee turned around before she realized the girl was making fun of her.

Aimee had told her mother, "I don't want to go to a new school. I'll never make friends."

"No, just kidding," the girl added quickly. "Yes, you. You're new, aren't you? We heard we were getting a new girl in our class. I'm Vanessa. This is Bridget."

The other girl leaned forward, smiled, and did a little wave thing.

Maybe her mother was right.

Give it a chance.

"I'm Aimee," Aimee said.

Vanessa scooched closer along the wall and Bridget followed, like they were attached by an invisible rope.

"Where are you from? Why weren't you here last week when school started? Did you just move here?" Vanessa asked in rapid-fire succession.

Aimee didn't know which question to answer first. "I had a bat mitzvah to go to over the weekend, so we just thought it would be easier to fly here after that," she said. She waited a beat, trying to think, and then added, "From Chicago. I'm from Chicago."

"Oh, cool," Vanessa went on. "Why did you move? Is your dad in the movie business? Everyone out here is in the movie business or something related to the movie business. My dad is a screenwriter. Is that why you moved?" She talked really fast.

"My dad is a script adviser," Bridget said quietly.

"Yeah, he works for Spyglass," Vanessa added. "So, what about your parents? Is that why you moved here? Isn't it so cool?"

Aimee hadn't thought it was cool at all.

She had begged her parents not to move, even going as far as leaving sticky notes all over the house, in secret places that they would find over the course of days or weeks. The laundry room, the coffee cupboard, her dad's bike, her mom's box of hair color. But nothing worked. This was a big opportunity for her mom, a promotion.

Her mom wasn't an actress or a director or a costume designer. She worked in finance, for a company called Cantor Fitzgerald, and her dad was a math teacher, so he was interviewing at schools in the area. The idea was that this new job of her mom's would change their lives for the better.

"It will make things easier," she'd heard her mother say. "For all of us."

"No," Aimee told the girls. "We moved here for my mom, but she's not in the movie business. She's in banking."

When she said that, Aimee could see their faces drop. Banking was boring. Vanessa was glancing off to the left. Bridget was already studying her nail polish. The thick scent of the tree blossoms was beginning to border on nauseating.

"But it's a really big job," Aimee rushed on. "It's so important that my dad doesn't even have to have a job."

That didn't come out right, but it was too late.

Vanessa's expression went from boredom to pity.

"Oh, I'm sorry. Your parents are getting divorced?"

"I'm so sorry," Bridget piped up.

"No, I didn't say that," Aimee blurted out.

Vanessa was shaking her head. "You didn't have to. That's the other thing about California. People move here just to get divorced."

And lunch period was over.

September 10, 2001
9:48 a.m. EDT
Brooklyn, New York

There was no way Sergio was going to school today. No way. Not after what had happened that morning when Paul decided to show up. Sergio needed some time to cool off, cool down. All the muscles in his body were tight, wound up, like twisted wires about to break. The image of Paul standing in the hallway kept flashing in Sergio's head, and he needed it gone. Sitting in a classroom wasn't going to cut it. Fresh air was the only answer. Fresh air to blow away the sight of his father—of Paul standing with his hands in his pockets, standing in the doorway. Waiting.

Sergio didn't refer to Paul as his father. He was Paul Kinkaid, and somehow he'd gotten wind of Sergio's math award and the trip to Chicago. He came by, early that morning, to congratulate his son. Couldn't a father congratulate his own son?

How did he find out?

It sure couldn't have come from Sergio's grandmother.

To say Nana wasn't fond of Sergio's dad was an understatement. He didn't ring the buzzer outside. He somehow managed to talk someone into letting him in, and he showed up at their apartment door. Knocking. Ringing. Calling out.

"Serge. It's me, Sergio. It's your dad. Sergio, open up."

"What do you want, Paul?" Nana said when she opened the door, but not all the way. She blocked the space between outside and inside with her own body. Paul kept trying to look past her, for his son.

"So, Sergio, I hear you are some kind of math genius."

The way Paul said it was like an insult.

Sergio didn't answer. His grandmother did. "Yes, as a matter of fact, he is," she said. "Is that all you wanted to know?"

She remained by the door. She didn't invite Paul inside. She didn't run to the kitchen and put up a pot of coffee, as she would for pretty much anyone else, including the UPS man, if he'd come by.

"No, I didn't come because I want anything."

Paul stood, his head nearly touching the doorframe. He was probably six feet three inches tall. It was the one thing Sergio hoped he would inherit from his father.

Paul turned to look at Sergio. He dug into his pant pocket. "I actually came to give him something."

Sergio would kick himself later. He would kick himself every single time it happened.

When would he realize not to expect anything? Not to trust Paul and never to let his guard down? But he did, and for a moment, for that single split second, Sergio thought his father had really gotten him something.

A gift? A card? Money? Money was always nice. Something to commemorate his accomplishment. It was what parents did, right? Parents who couldn't show up at the ceremony in Chicago might buy a gift, might slip their kid a little money. That was a reasonable thing to expect, right?

Sergio told his heart to be quiet, but instead his rebellious heart quickened with anticipation. Not for the money or the card or the gift, but the connection. His brain braced itself for certain disappointment, but his heart was ready to be evacuated of all previous sadness and make plenty of room for everything to be good, and real, and safe.

Like father and son.

Like, *Okay, you haven't been the best dad, but here you are now and you're trying to make it up to me because I'm your flesh and blood and because I love you. And because you love me.*

Those were all images Sergio now needed to erase. He felt a chill ripple down his spine, as if trying to shake itself loose from the past, even though the day was starting to get warm and sticky, like it was going to rain any minute, though so far it hadn't.

Sergio kept his hoodie on.

He had spent the better part of the morning wandering Brooklyn, far enough out of Red Hook not to be spotted by anyone he knew. He knew of kids who had been seen and dragged back to school. They dumped you right into detention anyway.

What was the point of that?

The fresh air was working. It was picking up the memories and sending them off into the blue sky. However, Sergio's sudden decision to fly down the subway stairs was less made than forced on him. He was certain that was the principal walking down Atlantic Avenue, and even though it didn't make sense, because she would be in school right now, lecturing some kid on his choice of clothing and explaining what self-respect meant, Sergio still panicked. He turned completely around and headed down into the tunnel. He swiped his MetroCard, but the turnstile didn't budge. Sergio could hear the train getting closer, hissing into the station. He swiped again. It didn't have any rides left. The underground train slowed and the doors were about to open. Above was the principal (maybe) and Paul (somewhere) and all the times Sergio had waited for his father to be his father.

Down here was emptiness.

Paul had stood there half in the doorway, searching around in his pocket for a while. Later, when he thought about it, Sergio wondered if Paul had actually been trying to come up with some kind of lie about how he had lost it. Or better yet: *It was right here in my pocket; someone must have stolen it. On the subway. Because now that I think about it, I remember I felt someone bump into me.*

Or had he really been looking for something?

Something that might be considered valuable in a third-world country by a kid who had grown up in a dump—like a nickel, a piece of gum still wrapped, a book of matches. And if he had found something like that, would he really have tried to pass it off as a gift?

It wouldn't be the first time.

* * *

Underground, Sergio could hear the train coming to a stop. His card didn't work, but he needed to catch that train. He needed to get across to the platform, but he didn't have any money, and if he thought about it one second longer, he'd chicken out.

Sergio looked cautiously to his left and then his right.

Oh, c'mon. Do it! Kids jumped the turnstiles all the time. No biggie. No one ever got caught, or rarely.

There wasn't a ticket booth at this station, so there was no MTA worker who might care too much about his job. No one. Just passengers. No one in blue, no cops that he could see. No one would even care.

Just do it.

Sergio had a choice—over or under? Sergio put a hand on either side of the turnstile, pressed down, tucked his knees to his chest, and in one smooth motion lifted himself to the other side.

Done. The train came to a full stop and the doors flew open, but just as Sergio was about to step inside, a strong hand on his shoulder pulled him back.

"There's a hundred-dollar fine for fare evading. You have any ID?"

Everyone else got on. The doors shut right in front

of him, and Sergio was alone on the platform with what, he then realized, must be a plainclothes officer. This day had gone from bad to worse.

That morning, when Sergio's father had pulled his hand out of his pocket, it was empty. He couldn't even come up with something to masquerade as a gift.

"I'm sorry, Serge."

"That's about right," Sergio's grandma said. "That's just about what I'd expect you to give your own son. Nothing."

Sergio didn't say anything.

Sergio was tired from yesterday, too tired to care. The flight from Chicago had felt long; the wait in the airport for the bus, the ride in the bus to Port Authority (was there any uglier place in the world?), and then the subway ride home had left him exhausted. Then Paul showed up at six thirty in the morning.

Bearing—what?

No gifts.

And still the oddest, tiniest rise of anger surfaced when his grandmother talked to his father like that. It wasn't anger at his grandma, who was all he had in the world, but at the world itself. The whole world and everyone in it.

"Great, so now that we've got that out of the way, you can leave." Sergio's grandmother puffed out her chest.

Paul looked defeated, like he really wished he had something to give his son. His shoulders sagged even more than they normally did.

"I heard about your trip, but I didn't know you were coming back so soon," Paul tried.

"Well, now you do," Sergio's grandmother said. She hadn't shut the door. Sergio could see out into the tiled hall. Mrs. Peterson was stumbling by, pushing her folded grocery cart in front of her. If she wanted, she could see right into their apartment, into their lives.

Sergio looked away. He wished Paul would leave already. The world did not need to be looking in. But that's the way it always was. Sergio on the inside looking out. Or was he always on the outside looking in? What difference did it make?

"So, Sergio won this big award? I'm really proud of him, you know. Just because I don't live here doesn't mean I'm not proud of him."

Something was wrong, Sergio could feel it. This was taking too long. Paul was standing too still. Paul never stood still. He shook and tapped and paced, and his hands flew all over the place. His eyes shifted. His weight shifted.

No, it can't be.

He wouldn't ask that, would he?

Paul could just stop right now and leave. It was bad enough he was here pretending to care, pretending to be interested in Sergio's life. *Just stop and walk away.* But he didn't stop.

"So, they paid for him to fly all the way to Chicago. Did they pay for his hotel? I hope it didn't cost you anything, Maureen."

Why? Why does he have to do this?

Sergio felt his heart constrict with a terrible rage, a blackness that clogged his ears, like being underwater. He didn't notice how tightly he was clenching his teeth until they began to hurt. His jaw ached.

He shouldn't feel responsible for the ugly, stupid thing Paul was going to say. He didn't need to worry about Nana and how upset she was going to be. For sure, his grandmother was a hundred times stronger than he was. Sergio didn't need to feel the pain when his own father asked if he had won any money.

But he would feel all those things.

He did.

"Did they award him any money for all the trouble? For all that work you had to go through, getting there and all? I bet they wouldn't have had such a fancy award ceremony if the winners didn't show up."

Sergio's grandmother was speechless. Her mouth was moving, but no sound came out.

Her eyes were speaking.

Get out. Get out of my house now before I disembowel you with my teeth and spit you out into the street for the rats to feast on.

Get out of my house.

But Paul couldn't see, couldn't hear it. Sergio noticed his father's eyelids drooping, and he watched his hand wander back, feeling for the doorframe.

"You know, if Sergio won anything, it's partially mine," Paul continued. His expression darkened. "By law it would belong to me."

Had his father really just said that?

Owed to him by law?

Did Paul really believe that he could possibly be entitled to money that didn't exist, from a math contest he'd only just found out about? Sergio thought for a second that Nana was going to clobber Paul with the coffee mug she was holding. Instead she just threw him out, and Sergio headed off. To school.

But then, not exactly.

And now, ironically, here was the law, with its hand on Sergio's shoulder.

September 10, 2001
10:07 a.m. EDT
Columbus, Ohio

"Naheed, what are you doing? We're going to be late for science." Eliza had walked past and been heading down the hallway when she stopped and looked back.

Naheed was fiddling with her locker. The combination had to be dialed and clicked in perfectly, or it didn't open and you had to start all over. This was probably why most kids just carried their books around with them all day. There wasn't enough time between periods anyway, even when your locker was cooperating.

"I need my science book." Naheed didn't take her eyes off her lock, starting over. Twenty-five. Fifteen. Thirty-two. That was the number, wasn't it?

"You go ahead. Don't worry about me," Naheed told Eliza.

In fact, please go ahead.

For some reason, even though Naheed and Eliza had never been friends before, Eliza had attached herself to Naheed this year, sort of like a new puppy. And sort of in a reciprocal way—even though it was annoying—Naheed didn't mind, because sixth grade was so much more confusing than fifth had been, and as strange as she was, Eliza seemed to know what to do and where to go in this unfamiliar maze of hallways and classrooms.

At the same time, Naheed really didn't want to stand out any more than she already did because she was Muslim and because she wore a head scarf.

And right now Eliza wasn't helping that cause.

"No, really," Naheed said, focusing harder on her locker. "Just go. You'll be late."

Eliza took the heavy steps back toward Naheed. "No, no. I'll wait. You probably need me to show you the way."

That was nice of Eliza, even if Naheed wished she wouldn't stand so close. Everyone knew Eliza was a little weird. She wasn't too clear on personal space. But the funny thing was, up until this year no one had really cared, or if they did, it wasn't necessarily a bad thing. Then middle school started last week and everything felt different, as if you suddenly realized you had been coming to school in your pajamas and you had to figure out a way to hide this fact before anyone else noticed.

It seemed Eliza wasn't going anywhere until Naheed finally got her locker to pop open and yanked out her science book.

"Okay, let's go."

Naheed hurried down the hall with Eliza, and just before Mrs. Salinger could close her classroom door, they managed to slip inside and drop into their seats.

"Nice you could join us, girls." Mrs. Salinger walked over to her place behind her desk. "As I was saying: We are going to use the scientific method to test these hypotheses. After every experiment, you will be required to write up your results." Mrs. Salinger stood up, a stack of papers in her arms. "Here is the format you will be expected to follow."

Eliza's hand shot up. "Can we work in pairs?"

That was her question, every time.

"Yes," Mrs. Salinger answered.

If gambling were allowed in her religion, which it was not, Naheed would have bet what was coming next, because lately it seemed that the universe was conspiring against her. In fact, just that morning Naheed had gone to pour her favorite cereal, only to find out her sister had eaten the last of it. But in the short run, what she ate for breakfast wasn't going to be the deciding factor. No, surviving middle school seemed to be predicated solely on who your friends were. And weren't.

Sure enough, Mrs. Salinger went on, "And I have already chosen the pairs, so don't bother begging. In fact, don't ask. The pairs are listed at the top of this sheet."

"But, Mrs. Salinger—" Eliza kept going.

Didn't she know resistance was futile?

Mrs. Salinger just ignored her.

"Take one and pass it back," she said. She counted out, exactly, the number needed for each row of seats.

It wasn't that Eliza was so awful or anything. She just talked a lot, even and especially when she had nothing interesting or important to say. And she said things that were really odd. Things most people only thought but knew better than to say out loud.

Now this year there was a whole batch of new kids from different elementary schools combined, and Naheed swore she could feel everyone jockeying for position, like horses on a racetrack. The truth was, Eliza didn't have any real friends, and being associated with her wasn't going to put Naheed anywhere near the head of the pack.

But the harder Naheed prayed to Allah that her

name would be coupled with someone, *anyone*, else, the more sure she was that Eliza's name and hers would be on the list side by side.

Because it was a selfish prayer, and selfish prayers don't get answered.

A second later it was confirmed when Naheed was handed the work sheet: "Pair Seven: Naheed Mohamadi/ Eliza Grayson."

Mrs. Salinger said, "You will need to come up with an experiment as a pair, run your experiment as a pair, and write up your results—"

"Do we have to be in pairs?" one boy shouted out from the back of the room.

Mrs. Salinger ignored him. "Come up with your experiment as a pair," she repeated as if she hadn't heard him at all. She wrote the first hypothesis out on the board: "Sensitivity is heightened on your dominant side."

There was a short discussion as to what "dominant side" meant.

No, not who was bossier. Not who weighed more.

No, it was meant to determine if you were right brained or left brained, usually connoted by handedness.

All that the pairs were expected to do today was to come up with their experiments. Tuesday they would have to get them approved. They had the rest of the week to implement their experiments, and by Friday their final reports were due. Chairs and desks were shifted around so the pairs could work together. Finally, everyone was settled and ready to begin.

Sort of.

"What is your dominant side, Naheed? What kind of name is Naheed, anyway? I've never known anyone else with that name."

It was starting right away, like it always did with Eliza. You would think that she was really lonely and had been storing up all these questions so she could make friends, only she'd ask the exact thing that made people not want to be friends with her. She wasn't anything like Nouri, but nonetheless she made Naheed think about her sister.

Maybe people felt that way about Nouri, too.

Whenever someone asked Nouri something about being Islamic, she sprang into action like she was a Sunday-school teacher. It wasn't that Naheed was ashamed of her religion or her family, but she didn't need to wear her beliefs on her sleeve—or her head—any more than she already did.

"It's a perfectly normal name," Naheed answered. She could practically hear her sister's voice in her head.

Naheed is a Persian name. It means "honorable and

blameless." Our family is not Arabic, but we are Muslim. We follow the practice of Islam. A lot of people think those two words mean the same thing, but they don't.

Always teaching.

We are Muslim and we follow Islam. It's like saying you are Christian and you practice Christianity. Does that make sense?

Enough already.

Naheed knew that she, too, had probably sounded exactly that way when *she* was nine and had first started wearing the hijab.

It shows that we are modest. That we are not looking for attention. It shows our devotion and loyalty to Islam. It's a command from Allah.

It was just that lately Naheed felt that wearing her hijab was more like showing she was different from everyone else. She certainly didn't need to explain it everywhere she went.

"I didn't say it wasn't normal," Eliza went on. "I just said I never heard it before and I wondered what the etymology of your name is."

"The *what*?"

"The origin of my name is Hebrew. It comes from Elizabeth, which means 'pledged to God.' Do you believe in God?"

"I think we better stick to the experiment," Naheed said. She opened her notebook. "Any thoughts? I think maybe try pricking people's finger with a pin. Or pinching them really hard and seeing which hand hurts more."

"That's not very scientific," Eliza answered.

"Well, do you have any better ideas?"

Sometimes Eliza did funny things with her face, tensing her mouth, blinking her eyes a lot. Naheed hadn't really ever noticed that before, but then again, she had never really spent this much time with Eliza, or been this close. They had never had a class together.

Eliza looked down at her hands. "I'm left handed," she said. "Well, really I can use both hands, but I write with my left hand. I throw with my left hand, but I wink with my left eye, and if you are left-hand dominant, you are supposed to wink with your right."

At the set of desks next to them, Tommy and Sebastian were wadding up pieces of paper and throwing them into a wastepaper basket, using the left hand, then the right.

Mrs. Salinger was pacing the room, but she stopped at their desk and asked the boys, "And exactly how does that indicate sensitivity?"

Tommy had some explanation about shooting

hoops, but Mrs. Salinger wasn't buying it, even though it sounded pretty reasonable to Naheed.

"Try again, boys," Mrs. Salinger said. She tapped her watch. "You have exactly eight minutes left."

Naheed looked up at the clock over the doorway, the second hand snapping in rhythm. Now they had seven minutes and fifty-two seconds.

"Cold water," Naheed said suddenly.

"Yeah, and we can time which hand you can keep in the cold water longer," Eliza said. "What do we need?"

"A timer."

"And ice cubes. And a big bowl."

Six minutes. Both girls were writing on their work sheets.

Eliza looked up. She was done. She smiled at Naheed. "Why do you wear that head covering?"

Naheed tried to ignore her. It had worked for Mrs. Salinger with that boy in the back of the room. She pretended to be still working on her work sheet.

"Huh? Why do you?" Eliza continued, a little louder, as if the reason Naheed hadn't answered had to do with a hearing problem. "Is it the same as how my nana keeps her head covered with a wig or a big scarf? She's Orthodox. Is it like that?"

Naheed looked around the room to see if anyone else was listening.

She didn't want to talk about her hijab.

Anyone else would have figured that out. And stopped asking.

But not Eliza.

Next to them, Tommy and Sebastian were still balling up paper, although now they were using it like a stress ball and seeing which hand could squeeze it tighter.

"Do you *have* to wear it?" Eliza went on.

If Naheed didn't say something, the whole class was going to start looking this way, and just because they had seen Naheed's head covering for three years didn't mean they understood. Or didn't notice.

But it was too late. Tommy and Sebastian seemed more interested in anything else than in their science experiment.

"Yeah, Naheed. Why do you have to wear that? Isn't it hot under there?" Tommy asked.

It wasn't.

Sebastian laughed. "I remember in third grade when you first wore it. I thought you had lost all your hair, like you were sick or something. Isn't that crazy?"

Yes. In fact, Naheed had long and very thick black

hair. It was one of the things she loved about herself. It was just like her mother's.

"So why do you, Naheed?" Eliza asked one more time.

Wearing pajamas to school might have been better than this. The last thing she wanted to do was explain *why*. It was as if all of a sudden Naheed was a giant in the room with an endless skein of cotton on her head and everyone was staring at her, and it.

"I don't know, Eliza," Naheed said. "Why do you have to be so annoying?" Which seemed to do the trick—the questions stopped—but it also sent Tommy and Sebastian into full-out hysterics.

And then Eliza looked like she was about to cry.

"Annoying Eliza." Tommy laughed. "That's a good one, Naheed."

Eliza's mouth was twitching more than ever and tears were filling up her eyes. Naheed had never seen anyone start to fall apart so quickly.

Sebastian echoed the sentiment. "Yeah, that's a good one."

The boys said it in unison and repeated it a few times for good measure, like a Greek chorus. "Annoying Eliza. Annoying Eliza."

The attention had shifted and Naheed could feel

herself returning to her normal size, but she also felt really bad. Eliza hadn't done anything wrong. She was just trying to make friends and she didn't know how.

The boys were still laughing.

Five minutes left.

Life science couldn't be over fast enough.

September 10, 2001
11:16 a.m. EDT
Shanksville, Pennsylvania

"Are you going to eat those?" Ben righted his chair back onto its four legs and leaned in toward Will's french fries.

When Will didn't answer, Ben helped himself, nabbing a handful of fries from Will's tray. The very familiarity of his bad manners was a relief, because for a long time after the accident had happened, even Will's best friends had acted differently around him. They wouldn't grab food off his plate. They didn't tease him, punch him in the arm, or give him dead legs in the dugout. Like he was too fragile. As if he would break. Like he was different somehow. And he supposed that was true.

After so many weeks and months, most people had

stopped telling him how sorry they were to hear about his dad, stopped looking at him like he had a toad on his head or something equally as unfortunate. And that was a relief too, because it was as if he had been hearing, through their apologies and condolences and cards and flowers and food and tears, something else they weren't saying.

He should have just kept driving past.

Or just called it in on his CB. Don't all truckers have CBs?

It didn't have to happen, did it?

Only, as the world outside his home began to forget, it brought a new sense of loneliness. It created a gap between "them" and "us," before and after, the haves (a dad) and the have-nots (a dad).

"Where's the ketchup?" Ben asked.

Alex tossed an unopened packet of Heinz across the table. "What are you looking at, Will?" he asked.

When he heard his name, Will whipped back around. "Nothing."

It wasn't until he saw Ben and Alex staring at him oddly that Will realized he had been searching the cafeteria for Claire.

She hadn't been on the bus this morning.

Was she absent? Maybe she was sick?

Or, Will guessed, she could have gotten a ride to school.

Maybe Claire wasn't on the bus because she had ridden her bike to school. It had been drizzling, but it was warm and not too wet. Perfect for bike riding. Will could have ridden to school. He *should* have. He had been thinking of doing that himself, lately.

It had nothing to do with Claire, of course.

He just thought he might want to ride his bike one of these days, before it got cold, before winter swooped in and hung around till March or April.

"Will, pay attention," Alex demanded. "I'm talking here."

"What?" Will refocused his attention back to the table.

"I was saying I have the new Madden," Alex went on. "You guys want to come over after school?"

"Cool," Ben said. "I'll bring a controller."

They both waited for Will's approval.

"Nah, I don't feel like it," Will said.

Since when had he stopped wanting to play video games?

"You guys can, though," Will added.

Since when? Since he didn't feel like doing much of anything anymore.

"Well, no, we can do something else if you want," Alex said quickly.

A year ago they would have just played Madden with or without him. Ben had been waiting months for this game to come out. Alex had preordered it.

No, his friends hadn't forgotten. Not completely. Not at all. Someone must have talked to them about the right way to behave when somebody's father died. Was killed.

Whatever.

"Yeah, we can play Madden anytime," Alex added.

But nobody got it right. Because there was no right.

"What do you feel like doing, Will?" Ben asked.

Will looked up and across the room.

What did he feel like doing?

He felt like sitting next to his dad in his old truck on the way to the dump on Sunday morning. He felt like getting up early and watching his dad try to make breakfast, crack the eggs and drip them all over the counter. He felt like throwing a ball in the backyard, back and forth, back and forth, until the rhythm of the ball hitting the leather and swooshing as it returned was all he could hear, and all he could feel. Until he and his dad were like one single unit.

But that's not the way things were.

"I don't know." Will shrugged.

Across the way a loud shriek of girly voices flew up into the room. So Claire *was* in school. She was there, sitting with her friends. Their faces lit up with laughter at something one of them had just said. The girls kept their seats close together, their heads almost touching as they giggled and talked.

There were only twenty-seven kids in the whole seventh grade, and Will had been in class with Claire in second, third, and fifth. They had ridden the same bus to school together every single year for eight years. But this year she looked different. She looked like a whole other person than the one he remembered. She looked, well, like a girl.

When she had heard he was going to Florida with his family, Claire had plopped down on the bus seat next to him. She said she had gone to Disney World before, and she let him in on which were the best rides at what time, and which ones to avoid altogether. She told him to bring sunscreen and lots of water, so he didn't have to buy it when he got to the Magic Kingdom.

"Because everything is so crazy expensive once you get into the park."

And Will didn't hear a word she said, but he noticed her hair and her smile and the faint smell of maple syrup when she was this close.

For a short time in fourth grade Will and Claire had actually been boyfriend and girlfriend. The whole thing was arranged by their friends, by delivering a note and returning to their side with the answer. Will agreed to be Claire's boyfriend, but by the end of the day she broke up with him, via another note, which read, "I don't want to be your girlfriend anymore. I'm sorry because you are a nice boy."

That would have been from the before. He was in the after. This was the now.

Will shifted his reverie away from the table of girls. "I feel like riding my bike," he blurted out.

Alex and Ben were silent for a beat. Then Ben said, "Okay, fine. Great. Good by me."

"Yeah, we haven't done that in a long time." If Alex was disappointed, which he probably was, he was good at hiding it. "It'll be fun," he said.

"What'll be fun?"

None of them had noticed that Claire was walking by with her tray, but they all looked up at the sound of her voice. She stood by their table and waited for their answer. Somewhere between fourth grade and this year Claire had gotten really pretty.

Ben and Alex answered at the same time, Ben saying "Nothing" and Alex saying "Biking," and it came out sounding like "Nubiking." Then Alex punched his knuckles into Ben's upper arm.

"Ow, what was that for?"

"So what is it?" Claire asked again, as if she kindly hadn't noticed any of their fumbling and nervousness. "What's so fun that you haven't done in a long time?"

Ben punched Alex back.

"Bike riding," Will spoke up. "We're just going to bike over to the old strip cuts after school." And then Will surprised everyone, himself most of all, when he added, "So you wanna come with us?"

September 10, 2001
11:18 a.m. PDT
Los Angeles, California

Of course it was so silly and just a big misunderstanding. Aimee knew her parents weren't getting divorced. They had been bickering a lot lately, but wasn't that just stress over moving, selling the house, and trying to find something in Los Angeles they could afford?

Sure, sometimes they argued over how much time Aimee's mother was working, who didn't do the dishes, who left the milk out all night.

But that would settle down.

Lunch period was long past; it was almost eleven thirty and now Aimee *was* hungry, but she had to find her next class. The inside of the school looked like a maze of stucco walls, each hall exactly like the one she had just come down, or turned around in and walked back the other way. The bell rang, and the doors were all closed by the time she found the room number that was marked on her slip of paper.

Her mother had been wrong about one thing: Missing school orientation was not a minor thing.

"Oh, sweetie. We can't fly to L.A. for the start of school and back for your cousin's bat mitzvah and back again a week later. It's not a big deal to start late. They don't do anything the first few days of school anyway. Right, Steve?"

She looked at Aimee's dad for confirmation, but he didn't give it.

"It's hard enough starting a new school," her father said. "Missing the first few days won't help."

"Well, *you're* not helping," her mother said, and maybe her voice was getting a little loud. "What do you want us to do? Fly back and forth? And who's going to pay for it? The flights alone would cost . . ."

Aimee shook the memory out of her head and tried to concentrate on algebra. She was supposed to be taking a test for her math placement, a test everyone else had taken last week.

What did she care what two girls she didn't even know thought about her?

Or her family?

What could they know?

Aimee looked down at her test and then up at the rest of the kids sitting at their desks. There were some things that were the same as at her old school—the desks, for instance. The desks were the same plasticky wood with the metal frame and the chair attached. And the white-board in the front of the room. And the teacher. The teacher kind of looked like Mrs. Franklin from fourth grade.

That was the year Aimee's mom first started working.

"I'm terrified," she'd confided in her daughter. Aimee's mom had been trying on outfits for her interview, and so far seven dresses, ten shirts, and three pairs of pants had landed on the floor. Various shoes, stockings, and socks were scattered in between.

"You'll be great, Mom." Aimee lay on her mother's big bed while her mom stood in front of the full-length mirror, this time in black slacks and a gray top. She held a pair of gold earrings up to the sides of her head. "What do you think?"

Aimee shook her head. "Not those," she said.

"No?" Her mother put the earrings down on the dresser and picked up another pair.

"Let me." Aimee bounced off the bed. Usually things went the other way around, with Aimee trying something on and asking for her mother's approval. This was exciting. If this new job meant they would spend more time together like this, like two best friends, like two girlfriends, Aimee was all for it.

Her mom stripped off the top and tried on something else. "I think I need to match the shoes to the jewelry, don't you?"

"Yeah, maybe," Aimee answered.

In truth, Aimee had no idea. Her mom was beautiful no matter what she was wearing. And all these dresses and earrings looked pretty much the same. Her mom seemed to favor blacks and grays, sometimes browns or olives. She called them earth tones. She looked good in everything she put on.

Aimee picked a scarf from the ones hanging on the inside of her mother's closet door. "How about this?" She held it out. "Instead of that necklace."

Her mother took off the necklace and tied the loose scarf around her neck. It did look good. The material of the scarf had a bit of all the colors her mom was wearing and a little burst of purple that pulled it all together.

"Oh my goodness, Aimee. It's perfect. You're a lifesaver."

Her mom scooped her into her arms, scarf and all, and hugged her, way too tightly, but Aimee remembered it as one of the happiest afternoons. They spent another half an hour cleaning up all the mess, hanging up shirts and dresses, and refolding pants, and then they went down to make dinner together. Meatless tacos, Aimee's favorite.

And they might even have baked cookies that night. Yes, Aimee was pretty sure they had. Oatmeal chocolate chip with raisins.

"How are you doing with that exam?" the Mrs. Franklin look-alike was asking.

"Oh." Aimee looked up. "Fine, I guess."

The teacher smiled and gave her that kind, it's-okay-if-you're-not-the-smartest-kid-in-the-class look.

Maybe if Aimee hadn't been such a fashion guru, her mom would never have gotten that job and they would never have had to leave Chicago. And her mom wouldn't have to be away so much. She'd be home right now, so that when Aimee got off the bus, she'd be there to hear about every last second of her very first day of seventh grade.

Or better yet, they'd still be in their old house. No new school, new teacher, new town, new kids.

No impending divorce.

No, just kidding.

Either way, her mother would have remembered to

pack Aimee a snack before sending her off to school, as she was now most likely going to starve to death.

"How about you finish it tomorrow?" the teacher said, reaching for the test paper.

Aimee was about to answer. She was about to say that, no, she could do it. It was easy math; she'd learned it last year. But her stomach spoke instead, with a loud grumbling roar, and there was still a whole afternoon left of school.

September 10, 2001
12:10 p.m. EDT
Brooklyn, New York

"What are you talking about? I swiped my card," Sergio said. He twisted his body and tried to yank himself out of the officer's grip, which loosened but didn't let go. There was rage lingering on the surface that rippled like a wave awakened into motion.

"I watched you jump the turnstile, son."

Son? I'm sure not your son.

"Let go of me."

The man let go, as if daring Sergio to run.

But Sergio knew better than to run. You didn't run.

You had to give a cop your name. You had to cooperate. You had to give in. Give up. Answer to those who served and protected a world that had never served nor protected him.

They were allowed to stop you for no reason. They could throw you up against the wall and pat you down, say whatever they wanted. And if you resisted, if you said one single thing, moved the wrong way, answered back, they could haul you in and that would be the end of that.

That was the law.

Stop anyone. Like every black kid walking (or *running*? Forget it!) down the street, in his own neighborhood, down in the subway. The police were allowed to do whatever they wanted—tease, taunt, humiliate, shove, prod, provoke. Sergio's cousin Ralph had spouted tears that time when the cops grabbed him and ran their hands all over his legs, around his chest, up and down his arms, holding his head down so he couldn't look up, so he couldn't turn and see anything but the dark smothering of his own hoodie. Heavy, angry hands all over his body; loud, angry voices robbing him of his being, of being a human being.

"Are you going to wet your pants, little boy?" one of the cops said. "Want me to call your grammy for you?"

Ralph was huge, dark skinned, with short dreads. He looked sixteen but he was only eleven, and he cried like a baby.

No, Sergio was not going to cry. He was not going to bend. Not going to break.

"Where are you going so badly you need to steal a ride?"

"What's it to you?" Sergio answered.

I dare you. I just dare you.

"Look, I'm not a police officer. I'm not going to give you a ticket."

Sergio lifted his eyes from the concrete platform. "What the—"

"Engine 209. Ladder Company 10. Sorry, kid. I was just . . ."

He should have noticed the man wasn't wearing a vest. The guy was just jacked, broad-chested with strong, brown-skinned arms. He wasn't a cop. He couldn't do anything. He was just a fireman.

"I just thought . . . I just wondered why you weren't in school. I have a nephew your age. It's Monday." The fireman laughed. "But a good day to play hooky, I suppose. Hey, look, that's what I'm doing."

Sergio leaned in and looked for the next train. The tunnel was dark.

"I'm not skipping. My school has the day off." Sergio straightened himself up and answered where there was no question. They stood in silence for a long while.

"Well, technically, you know, I'm not either." The fireman seemed to feel the need to explain. "I swapped days with a guy in my company. And you wouldn't believe why."

The roar of the distant train whooshed into the station. A tiny light grew closer. Sergio had absolutely no interest in this guy or why he had the day off, but the unsettling sense of his authority lingered, as well a kind of yearning for it at the same time.

"Okay, I'll play. Why?"

The fireman smiled. "It's this guy's anniversary tomorrow, and he wants to surprise his wife. Take the day off, you know? So he's working my shift now, and I'll work his tomorrow, no big deal. But that's a nice story, right? Wanna tell me yours?"

No.

Sergio shook his head, and when the train stopped and the doors opened, he got in. The fireman, too. The doors hissed closed and the train lurched forward. The car was mostly empty. Across from him sat an old lady with a grocery cart folded and leaning against her legs. If Sergio didn't know better, it might have been Mrs. Peterson from his building, but this lady was Chinese. There was a white man in a business suit and tie playing with some little device in his hands, one of those PalmPilot things, tapping the screen with a skinny pen.

The subway hummed along, rocking rhythmically, like the washers in the basement did. Hummed so that girls in his apartment building sometimes put their babies up on top of the machines and let the vibrations lull them into sleep. The lights flickered for a second. The train started to slow and then sped up again, then slowed again, and black steel girders covered with years of oil and dirt became dimly visible outside the windows.

Sergio looked up and over at the fireman, who was sitting on the opposite side of the train, a bunch of seats farther down. The train jerked once more and then stopped altogether. The lights went out and the low emergency bulbs lit up. Everyone turned and looked out the windows at the blackness. And waited.

This was New York. It happened all the time. It could be thirty seconds. It could be thirty minutes.

After about five minutes the grocery lady tipped her head back and started snoring.

The businessman must have checked his watch at least a dozen times in the last minute, and then finally he let out a loud groan. But it didn't bring the train back to life.

Sergio stretched out his legs. What difference did it make? He didn't have anywhere to go. Though he wasn't thrilled about all this empty time to think. He didn't like thinking too hard, except about math. Math had no feelings. It never let you down. Math made sense. People did not. Sergio deliberately made sure not to look toward where the fireman was sitting, or make eye contact with him. No use inviting any more unwanted friendly conversation.

Another few minutes went by, snoring and time checking, checking time and snoring. But the train itself remained silent.

"I can't believe this. I just can't believe it," the white man suddenly said out loud. He stood up and walked over to the window on the other side of the train, as if he might be able to see the problem from that angle.

"It can't be much longer," the fireman said. He recrossed his arms, modeling patience for the impatient man.

"Easy for you to say." The man sat back down. "I have to get to work."

Sergio looked up.

What's that supposed to mean?

They were all stuck on the train. Why did this guy think he was the only one with someplace to go? Because he was *white*?

Another minute passed and the man jumped up again. "I can't take it." He headed for the door that led from one car into the next. He pulled on the handle, but it didn't open.

The fireman stood. "Sir, that's not a good idea. If the train suddenly starts moving . . . it's dangerous. You should probably stay seated."

"And who the hell are you?" the man shot back.

The tone of his voice was like a volt of electricity in Sergio's body, unpleasant, familiar. Without being aware of it, Sergio tightened his hands into fists.

What had his grandmother taught him? Stay out of fights. Stay away from men who fight. When you see a fight, turn, walk the other way.

There was nowhere to go, though. Nothing to do but sit and watch, still his body. Stay alert.

"I work for the city of New York. Now, will you kindly take your seat. Sir," the fireman answered.

The man yanked at the handle again. "The city of New York. Well, that explains a lot." He pulled harder, and suddenly the train lit up, bells were dinging, and the wheels screeched into motion, pitching the man forward. He hit his head hard on the door and slumped to the ground.

Only then did the grocery woman wake up.

"Oh my God. That man is bleeding!" she screamed.

September 10, 2001
2:45 p.m. EDT
Columbus, Ohio

Naheed's very first hijab had been a gift when she was nine years old, from her mother. That day, instead of feeling different, it made Naheed feel connected.

It made her feel grown-up and special.

Her first hijab was robin's-egg blue, the color of Naheed's own eyes. That night her mother showed her how to pull back her hair and slip the solid blue headband over her head. Then her mother lifted up the long, lovely scarf and gently folded it around and around, enveloping her daughter in tradition and love. She gave Naheed her own strawberry-shaped pincushion, and together they sat in front of the mirror, practicing, wrapping and unwrapping, pinning and unpinning, until they both were laughing, and until Naheed's own hands could nimbly fold and wrap and pin all by themselves, and until she looked almost as beautiful as her mother.

"Now you have your thinking cap on, Naheed," her mother said. "Do you know why I call it a thinking cap?"

Naheed had wrapped the scarf counterclockwise around her head. Her mother was left handed and had wrapped clockwise. When her mother had been demonstrating, they had worked like mirror images, their hands and arms in unison. Naheed was only nine then, but she knew the answer to her mother's question.

"Because when I observe hijab, I am always reminded who I am."

Her mother nodded and smiled. "That's good. That's right. Always remember you can wear the silkiest, most beautiful hijab in the world, but what matters is what's in here." She tapped her heart and then her head. "And here. And how you treat people. Yourself included, dear one."

Naheed couldn't wait to get to school and show everyone. All the girls wanted to know about it. They wanted her to show them how to put it on. They wanted to touch it. But that was then, fourth grade.

That was before the boys stopped including everyone in their recess basketball games. And before the end of fifth grade, when girls formed blockades to the bathroom during lunchtime, allowing some girls in, while others had to wait.

It was before middle school.

And that was before this afternoon, when a bunch of kids in the cafeteria started a slow chant, all because of what Naheed had started in an effort to take the attention away from her hijab. It wasn't what she'd intended, but now it was too late.

"Annoying Eliza. Annoying Eliza."

At first it was quiet, under their breath when Eliza walked by with her tray, but it seemed to follow her and get louder when she didn't react. Eliza kept her eyes straight ahead, as if she had been trained how to behave in these kinds of situations. She sat down alone, and eventually the collective caroling stopped. But when she got up to put away her tray, someone picked up the chant again, though not with quite the same zeal.

"Annoying Eliza."

Naheed wanted to bury her head, hijab and all, in the ground and hide. She wanted to tell everyone to stop. The right thing to do would have been to stand up and help Eliza, even if she hadn't been the cause of this whole mess. That would have been the right thing. Not to mention that she *was* the cause of it all, and Eliza looked so miserable.

And alone.

Instead Naheed sat at her table with her best friends, the three girls she had known since kindergarten. She sat with her back to the rest of the cafeteria, and she tried to eat her lunch.

Uncle Iman and Aunt Judith flung the front door wide open before Naheed could reach the handle.

"*Azizam*, you are home."

"Yes, Uncle."

"How was your day in school today?" he asked.

Naheed hadn't even slipped her shoes off yet. It was a trick question anyway. Uncle Iman didn't want his nieces in public school. He often fought with his brother about why he wasn't sending Naheed and Nouri to a Muslim school.

"Fine," Naheed answered, though of course nothing was fine.

Annoying Eliza.

Annoying Eliza.

Naheed ducked under her uncle's arms and dodged past.

"What kind of answer is 'fine'?" Uncle Iman turned and followed her into the kitchen. "Did you do prayers today?"

"Leave her alone, Iman," Aunt Judith tried.

That was a lot for her to say. Naheed's uncle was very observant, and he did not believe a wife should ever contradict her husband. Naheed's parents were nothing like that at all. The whole thing was very confusing, especially since Aunt Judith was a convert. She had not even been born into Islam.

"I am leaving her alone. I am just asking if she prayed today," Uncle Iman said, and they all walked into the kitchen.

Naheed's mother was at the sink. "She makes up her prayers at third prayer, Uncle Iman. Now go and get ready, Naheed. Nouri will be home soon. You can help her learn proper *wudu* tonight."

That seemed to quiet Uncle Iman.

And maybe it was what Allah wanted her to do. But it wasn't just your beliefs, her father had said many times, it was your behavior.

Maybe praying would help, but fixing things with Eliza was going to take a little more planning.

September 10, 2001
3:25 p.m. EDT
Shanksville, Pennsylvania

One by one, without piling on top of one another, Will, Alex, Ben, and Claire skidded to a fast stop, dropped their bikes by the side of Skyline Drive, and headed toward the giant draglines that had been left behind in the abandoned strip mine. It was still bright out, though the sun had shifted to the other side of the horizon, above the tops of the far line of trees. The light had that tinted orange look that meant fall would be coming soon, and then the darkness of winter. But for now the summer extended just a little bit longer, and all four of them ran across the open ground until they were out of breath.

"Wow, holy crud. They're so freakin' big." Alex stood at the top of a small hill of dirt, in the midst of a huge hill of dirt, cleared long ago and now stretching empty, except for the two pieces of mining equipment resting in the distance.

"They're massive," Ben said.

Claire put her hand up to her forehead to shield her eyes from the lowering sun. "They look like two knights bowing to each other."

They did. The two huge machines faced each other, with their tall metal booms stretched out at an angle, like two medieval horsemen with their long swords tipped forward. Or sentinels, keeping guard, waiting patiently and silently.

But only a girl would say something like that.

Or Will's dad.

When Will and his sisters were little, their dad would lie with them in the grass in their backyard, looking up at the sky, at the low clouds and the way they moved over the tops of the trees. It always looked like the earth was spinning so fast. If you stared at them long enough, you felt dizzy.

"I'm getting carsick," Will's sister Rooney said one time.

And they all laughed.

Will's dad would see things in the clouds that no one else ever could. Fantastical things. Amazing things.

Playful things that made the girls laugh, and magical things that made Will want to run inside and write stories about them.

Why did he do something so dangerous, so stupid?

Didn't he think about us when he got out of his truck?

Didn't he think about me*?*

Everyone called his dad a hero, but it didn't make sense. Heroes did heroic things, they saved lives, they pulled people out of burning buildings. They risked their lives to save others, but they didn't die doing nothing. Of course he knew his father had done a good thing, or had *tried* to do a good thing. But what had come of it?

"Hey, remember when we used to play WWF in your basement?" Will turned to Alex.

"Yeah, but what made you think of that?"

Anything to stop thinking about his dad.

"This!" Will took a flying leap from the small hill of earth he was standing on and landed on Alex's back. They both went down onto the loamy soil.

It was like old times instantly. Ben spread his feet apart, to ground himself, lifted an imaginary microphone to his mouth, and began the color commentary.

"And in this corner, weighing two hundred and ninety-five pounds, from Indian Lake, Pennsylvania . . .

it's the Earthquake, doing his signature move."

"Oh no," Alex yelled, laughing, but it was too late. Will bounced from invisible rope to invisible rope, as if gaining momentum. He sat right down on Alex's chest and stayed there, ostensibly holding him captive, while Alex flailed his legs and arms around helplessly. Ben slapped the ground, declaring Earthquake the winner.

"This is dumb," Claire said. She folded her arms over her chest and watched.

It was dumb, but they couldn't stop. Will couldn't stop. It was too much fun. The boys took turns refereeing, winning, losing, being beaten, twisted and torn, from dropkicks, the flying clothesline, and the ever-impressive flapjack spine crusher.

He was a kid again, and everything was going to be all right forever.

"Hey, let's do something else," Claire called out. "Someone's going to get hurt."

It wasn't like she was wrong about that. Back in the day, down in Alex's basement, Ben had once cut his head on the metal heating vent. Alex had gotten a rug burn so serious his mom had to take him to the doctor the next day. Will himself had gone home from their wrestling sessions aching, and wondering if he hadn't cracked a rib or two.

But it felt good to fight again. To fight back.

To play hard and mean it.

And not break.

"Hey, I'm serious," Claire yelled. "Stop!"

Somehow her complaints just egged the boys on. What was a good fight without an audience? The more upset Claire got, the more fun it all seemed. The harder they fought.

Will looked up from his face-plant. He could see that Claire was really getting annoyed. After all, he was the one who had asked her to come. And then Will remembered how many times he had thought about spending time with her.

But not like this.

It felt strange, like there were two halves to his body. One wanted to get up and hold Claire's hand and just sit and look out at the clouds and the sky, maybe even talk.

And who knows?

And the other half wanted to struggle and roll and sweat and twist this person's arm behind his back and not be worried about anything at all.

"I've had it," Claire said finally.

Will could see her getting up and walking away. In another second she'd be on her bike and heading back to her house, and in one more second she'd probably never want to talk to him again.

They always *had* needed someone to tell them when enough was enough. Usually when someone got a little hurt and Alex's mom came running down the basement stairs, telling everyone it was time to go home before someone got *really* hurt.

Or when Alex's little brother looked as if he might have gotten knocked unconscious for real and it was time to bribe him to keep his mouth shut.

Or when Claire was walking away, lifting her bike off its side, swinging her leg over, and leaving.

And she was gone.

September 10, 2001
2:10 p.m. PDT
Los Angeles, California

The last class of Aimee's first day at her new school was her least favorite, physical education. Aimee considered opting out by claiming low blood sugar from involuntary fasting, but she decided against starting out the year as the class hypochondriac.

Besides, everyone else looked so excited to be outside again in the scorching Los Angeles heat. She didn't want to call attention to herself. She figured she could just blend in. Although out here in the bright sun, which was reaching higher into the sky, the other students' hair looked even blonder. And in shorts, they all looked like Olympic track stars. Tan Olympic stars.

"Okay, everyone, you can socialize later. I'll give you time at the end of the period. Right now line up into the same teams we made last week." The gym instructor was a ridiculously good-looking young teacher named Tom Cruise.

For real.

But maybe it wasn't spelled that way.

Of course, Aimee had no idea where to stand as the other kids started to separate themselves into two teams, meandering their way to one end of the grassy area or the other. If she didn't move, she'd end up right in the middle, like a monkey, like a hot roasted monkey.

It wasn't *that* hot, to tell the truth. It was exactly as Aimee's mother had promised, mild and dry, perfect Southern California weather.

And where was her mother now? In New York City. Probably looking at studio apartments to rent for herself.

"Aimee. Over here!" a voice shouted. It was Bridget, minus Vanessa. Aimee could just make out what she was saying. "Come onto my team." Bridget was waving her arms and mouthing.

Aimee didn't need to be asked twice. She rushed over to her left and merged into the group of kids Bridget was standing with.

"Thanks," Aimee told her gratefully.

Gym turned out to be not so horribly bad, even on an empty stomach. In fact, it was kind of fun and it took

Aimee's mind off food. Bridget turned out to be pretty nice. They ran crazy relay races without winners, because that, apparently, was another thing about California: Everyone is a winner. When she caught her breath, Aimee thought about what she would tell her mother on the phone when she got home.

I think I might have made a friend. Her name is Bridget.

Until Vanessa showed up right before the end of the period, just when—as promised—Tom Cruise gave the class a few minutes to "socialize." Bridget and Aimee were sitting cross-legged on the ground.

"What are you two doing?" Vanessa sat down right between them, even though it would have made more sense for her to sit where there was much more room, next to Aimee.

Bridget had to shift over to make space. "Just talking," she answered ever so quietly.

"Are you in this class too?" Aimee asked Vanessa.

"Yes," Vanessa answered. "But I know what you're doing."

Bridget let her eyes fall, like there was something incredibly interesting crawling around there in the grass.

"Doing?" Aimee asked. "What am I doing?"

"You're reacting to your mom and dad splitting up

by trying to steal someone else's best friend. Mine. I see right through you."

The words were so nonsensical Aimee thought it must be some movie business tradition. The way boys were always reciting lines from movies. Maybe here in California, people did that all the time. Aimee tried to figure out what movie this could be from. *X-men*? *Star Wars*?

"No, she's not," Bridget tried. She kept her head down. "She was just telling me about her old school."

"I'm sure," Vanessa said. "Well, everybody knows what happens when the mom is more successful than the dad. Just look at Reese Witherspoon and Ryan Phillippe. How long do you think that's going to last? I mean, what has he even done since *Cruel Intentions*?"

She leaned in toward Aimee and asked, "Is there someone else? There's always someone else in cases like this."

Aimee ran to the phone as soon as she opened her front door and burst into her new house. What she *wanted* to do was cry and complain and wail and cry some more. What she really wanted was for her mother to be here, right here. Right now. After Aimee's very worst day in her entire life, hands down, no contest, worst day ever. She dialed her mother's mobile number.

"How was school, sweetie?" Her mom's voice sounded so far away. Three thousand miles far away. "I'm so sorry I wasn't there. But I'm sure it was great. I'm sure you were great."

And slowly, like the realization that you've just cut yourself on that seemingly harmless piece of paper, it *did* make sense what Vanessa had been saying. Her mom didn't really want to know about her day. She just wanted everything to be great. *Great.* So her mom didn't have to feel bad that she had to go away to this stupid meeting at the worst possible time for Aimee. Her mother didn't want to hear what had really happened, she just wanted to feel good about what she was doing instead of terrible, which was what she should have been feeling.

"Fine," Aimee answered.

It wasn't a very good mobile phone connection, which made it easier for Aimee to answer in monosyllables and not have to explain why. She didn't feel like talking to her mom right now. She sure didn't want to listen.

"So, I'll call you tomorrow morning before my meeting, okay, sweetie?" her mother was saying. "Before you head off to school again. Okay?"

"When?" Aimee asked.

"My meeting is at nine o'clock but it's all the way downtown," her mother told her. "It's in the World Trade

Center, so Chris and I have to leave the hotel around eight."

Aimee had never heard her mother mention anyone at work named Chris.

"Aimee, are you there? Aimee? Okay? I'll call before I leave for my meeting."

Chris?

"Mom, that's five in the morning here," Aimee heard herself saying. "I'll be sleeping."

"I know, sweetheart. So I'll just leave a message on the machine, like I always do. You don't have to pick up. I just want to say good morning and I love you. Okay?"

Aimee felt her throat sting.

"I love you, Aimeleh," her mother said into the phone.

And that's when Aimee was supposed to answer with the matching Yiddish nickname: *I love you, too, Mamaleh.*

"Aimee?"

"Can't hear you, Mom," Aimee said, holding the phone out, away from her mouth. "I gotta go."

And she hung up.

September 10, 2001
4:10 p.m. EDT
Brooklyn, New York

"My nana is going to be so crazy worried," Sergio said. He looked at the clock hanging on the wall behind the cash register. How had the whole day gone by so fast? It was past four. Since the accident on the subway he had been talking for hours, nearly nonstop, to Gideon.

Gideon looked at his watch. "Wow, you're right. It's late. I didn't realize what time it was." He paid the check and counted out five singles from the change. He walked back and laid them on the table where he and Sergio had just finished burgers, fries, and milk shakes.

He returned to where Sergio was surveying the gum and candy display under the counter while he waited. "Want me to call your grandma and explain?" Gideon asked.

There would be so much to explain. This morning felt like it had happened days ago: his dad in the doorway, skipping school, walking the streets, ducking into the subway, jumping the toll, the man bleeding from his head, and Gideon jumping into action. That had been like a movie. But it wasn't a movie. It was real. Sergio would never forget it. Now, when he was trying to remember it in detail, it felt like it had happened forever ago, but it had probably been only a couple of hours.

"Hey, hold still," Gideon ordered the man, who immediately tried to stand up again, reaching for the subway pole and missing.

Of course, Sergio didn't know Gideon's name yet.

"Hey, kid. Come here."

"Me?" Sergio said.

Gideon didn't bother answering that question. "Give me your T-shirt."

Sergio reflexively looked down at his own body. His hoodie was tied by the arms around his waist; he wore a beater, and a V-neck over that.

"The outer one. The T-shirt," Gideon yelled. "Give it to me."

Now that the man was sitting upright, the blood ran

freely from his head like a freaking river, covering his face in a red mask.

My T-shirt. Is this guy kidding?

New T-shirts were like gold, especially Ralph Lauren V-necks. They were not easy to come by. If he was lucky, Sergio found a three-pack at Marshalls. He even washed them by hand to make sure they lasted.

Gideon yelled, "Now," and this time Sergio obeyed. He tore off his hoodie and pulled his T-shirt over his head and tossed it to the fireman.

"Can you tell me your name?" Gideon spoke calmly to the man, as if nothing were unusual at all; at the same time he folded Sergio's brand-new, perfectly white tee into a square and pressed it to the guy's bloody head.

The man struggled. "My name?"

"Do you know where you are?" Gideon asked.

The man didn't answer, but he didn't try to stand again. He seemed totally out of it, losing his balance, nearly toppling over onto his side. His eyes were wide and darkening. His mouth moved, but nothing came out.

"You are on the subway. Just take a deep breath. Everything's going to be all right. You hit your head. We need to get you to a hospital."

The way he spoke, the confidence, the firmness, even the kindness of it, reminded Sergio of something long ago. Something he had lost. Something that wasn't his, but should have been.

"Listen, I am Gideon. I'm a firefighter. And a medic."

The subway raced through the tunnel and then jerked and hissed to a stop. The doors slid open. Gideon called to Sergio again.

"Come and help me get him to his feet. We need to call an ambulance."

At this point resistance was futile. Sergio didn't hesitate. Besides, he didn't want to. He wanted to be included in whatever was happening. So with Gideon on one side, still pressing the T-shirt against the wound, and Sergio on the other, they hoisted the man to his feet and made their way out of the train. The station was crowded with people.

"Please, everyone, move out of the way," Gideon called out.

They stepped in unison across the platform and lowered the man down onto a bench. Like the parting of the Red Sea, everyone moved out of their way. Sergio could feel Gideon's authority, only it wasn't threatening. It was powerful, and it was transferred by their connection. People listened and did what Gideon said, and now Sergio was part of that.

"Take my mobile phone." Gideon reached into his

back pocket. "Go up to the street and call nine-one-one."

Sergio took the phone, and even though he had known the number all his life, he repeated it to himself with every step he took.

"Emergency, please move. Emergency." Sergio imitated the commanding tone that Gideon had had in his voice, and people stepped out of the way without question. When he got up to the street, he pressed in the number.

"Nine-one-one. What is your emergency?"

"There's a guy here who hit his head pretty bad. He's bleeding and seems . . ." Sergio paused, searching for the right word that would be accurate, not hysterical, something urgent and intelligent, to bring immediate help.

"Incoherent," he said.

"Is he breathing?" the disembodied voice asked.

"I don't know. I think so. I had to come up here to call. Just send an ambulance."

"Where are you?"

That's when Sergio realized he had no idea where he was. He looked back at the subway entrance. "Bowling Green Station. The uptown platform."

"Emergency personnel have been dispatched to your location. Can you remain at the scene?"

"Yes."

"May I have your name, sir?"

Sergio didn't hesitate—the New York City dispatch wouldn't care if one twelve-year-old boy was skipping school, anyway.

This was more important. This mattered more than he did.

"Sergio Kinkaid Williams. I gotta get back down there."

As soon as he entered the station, the phone service cut out. Gideon was still at the bench. The man was lying down across it, moaning.

Gideon didn't ask Sergio if he had made the call, or if he had reached anyone. Gideon assumed he had.

"He's got a concussion. He's still bleeding. But he'll be okay."

Sergio could hear the sirens from the street above.

After the ambulance finally arrived, the paramedics came running down the stairs. There seemed to be some kind of brotherhood, some unspoken agreement, when they found out Gideon was a firefighter. And now Sergio was included, too.

"Hand me that bag, kid." One of the paramedics was on his knees and reaching out his hand.

Sergio lifted the medic bag and passed it over. He felt his heart pumping, adrenaline rocking his body.

Only when it was all over, when the paramedics had carried the man up the stairs strapped to a gurney, the ambulance doors had slammed shut, and the crowd had dispersed, did Sergio pause and remember who he was. Where he was. And why. At the same time it was as if a door had been cracked open, letting in light from the other side, from a hallway he had never seen before.

Gideon was pulling off his plastic gloves. He said to Sergio, "Guess I owe you a new T-shirt."

They stood on the street, facing in the direction the ambulance had driven, the sound of the siren wailing in the distance.

"Nah, it's okay," Sergio said.

Sergio didn't really care about the T-shirt anymore, but he didn't want this, whatever it was, to be over. He didn't want the door to shut just yet. He wanted to know more about what lay on the other side.

"I know it's okay, but I want to do it. C'mon, there's a store right over there."

"That's kinda weird," Sergio said, because it was.

"Well, here, I'm Gideon Burke." He put out his hand. "Oh, maybe I could call your mom and ask her permission. I could explain what happened?"

Ask her permission? That's a funny one, Sergio thought.

Nobody had been there to ask permission when he was living on the street. Before his nana found him.

Was it a day? A week? A month? There was conflicting information. In his memory there were only vague, shadowy images that might not even be real. People had quizzed him, had asked him so many questions that Sergio no longer knew what was a real memory, what was a dream, a nightmare, or somebody else's story he had picked up along the way.

But one thing in his memory was certain. They had been together then, Sergio and his mom—no one disputed that—living in a shelter in Albany. They shared a room. Was it white? Were there bunk beds? A dresser?

Food came at long tables, didn't it?

Plates divided into sections. Soapy, clean water. Was there a playroom with toys? Dirt on the faces of the plastic people, plastic action figures with missing eyes, hands, a missing leg. He remembered that.

Bent puzzle pieces. Broken boxes. Tiny, square orange carrots. Applesauce. White sheets. Men yelling. Milk in small containers. Blankets that were thin and too small to fit around them both, so his mother tucked him in and curled around him.

But the strongest memory that Sergio could attribute to either reality or desire was the smell of his mother, close to him, warming him, holding him, all the dark night.

Until they found her dead, according to reports. Had there been a child with her? It seemed to have gone unreported. Sergio was picked up on Route 32 in downtown Albany, and nobody would say for sure how long he had been wandering. It was the three-day hospital stay he remembered most.

Clean sheets. Warm-water sponge baths.

Ice cream every night.

And then they tracked down his maternal grandmother.

The grandmother, as it turned out, lived in New York City, in Red Hook, Brooklyn, and had been searching for her daughter for three and a half years, exactly Sergio's age. She never saw her daughter, but she held on to Sergio like a fierce hawk with tremendous talons.

September 10, 2001
9:45 p.m. EDT
Columbus, Ohio

That evening Naheed could not wash enough for *wudu*. Nouri was already finished. She didn't need any help remembering. Face, hairline to chin. Forearms, elbow to fingertips, right then left. Scalp.

And lastly, feet. Right foot with right hand. Left foot with left. Toes to ankles.

Nouri ran water over the tops of her socks and called it a day. But Naheed couldn't wash long or hard enough. Before you can pray, you need to wash. You need to be clean, not just of real dirt, but of all the bad things you might have done with your hands, your ears, your eyes, your mouth. Your words.

Annoying Eliza.

Annoying Eliza.

In her mind Naheed could see Eliza's sad face while she was trying to eat her lunch in the cafeteria, even though Naheed hadn't turned around to see her once. All Eliza needed was one friend and she could probably have handled the teasing. Maybe even laughed it off. But alone, it was a tsunami.

When Naheed crawled into bed that night, Nouri was already asleep. Naheed would get her own room back when Uncle Iman and Aunt Judith left the next day, but for now her little sister occupied the trundle bed right below.

Naheed's mother appeared in the doorway. "Are you all tucked in?"

Naheed answered, and her voice cracked when she spoke. "Yeah, I am."

Instead of moving away, her mother opened the door farther, letting light from the hall fall across the two beds, separating them right in half, light and dark. She stepped inside and sat down at the end of Naheed's bed, careful not to rustle Nouri. There was really no need. Nouri had been known to fall asleep right at the dining-room table at late-night suppers and stay sleeping while everyone cleaned up.

Some trick, that was.

"What's wrong?" Naheed's mother asked.

Naheed wanted to say: *Nothing*. Because she wanted that to be the truth. And because the last thing Naheed needed was for her little sister to hear any of this, she said as softly as she could, "Something bad happened today."

"Something bad?" her mother whispered back. She rubbed Naheed's feet under the blankets. "At school?"

Only, just as Naheed was going to tell her mother about how she had been mean to Eliza because she didn't want anyone to be mean to her, but then it had all gotten out of control and everyone started being mean to Eliza too, something entirely else came out of her mouth.

"Two boys were teasing me about my hijab," Naheed said.

"Oh? What did they say?" her mother asked.

"Well, one of the boys wanted to know if it was hot under my scarf all the time. And the other boy said he thought I went bald in third grade and that's why I had to keep my head covered."

Her mother was quiet for a moment.

"And what did you tell them?"

"Nothing." Which was sort of the truth.

"Nothing? You know we've talked about this, Naheed. People don't understand, and it's your job to show them that you are proud of who you are. And teach them, let them see that we are not like what they see on the television. And in the movies. You can do that, can't you?"

Naheed nodded. She could do that. She just hadn't. Because it was easier to have the unwanted attention on someone else than to have to explain.

All the time. And have people stare.

And ask more questions.

"Sometimes I wish I didn't have to be Naheed the Muslim girl. I wish I could just be Naheed."

Her mother laughed. "And who would that be?"

Naheed shrugged her shoulders up to her ears.

"Be strong. And don't let silly boys who tease you ruin your day." Her mother kissed her daughter on the top of her head. "There will be silly boys always. Their words cannot hurt you if you don't let them. If you know who you are. Now, tomorrow is Tuesday. A fresh start, right? And remember I have to leave for work early. So get some sleep now, okay?"

Naheed's mother lifted herself from the bed. "Good night, Naheed."

"Good night, Mommy."

"And good night, Nouri," their mother said.

Nouri didn't miss a beat. "Good night, Mommy," she answered. So Nouri had been awake the whole time.

Figures.

When their mother had left the room, Nouri sat up

and leaned over to her sister's bed. "Did they really think you were bald?"

"Yes, isn't that hysterical?" Naheed held out her hand to her little sister. It was actually nice to be able just to reach out and hold her sister's hand while they lay in their beds.

"With all your black hair?" Nouri scooted closer and petted her sister's head. She took a thick strand and let it slip through her fingers, around and around.

"Naheed?" Nouri said after a beat.

"Yeah?"

"I'm sorry you had a bad day."

"It wasn't so bad," Naheed said. "I can fix it tomorrow. At least I'm not bald."

And both sisters dived into their pillows, trying to muffle their giggles.

September 10, 2001
5:45 p.m. EDT
Shanksville, Pennsylvania

The ride home wasn't exactly the way Will had imagined it would be when he realized he had invited Claire to come bike riding with them. The boys rode three across, peddling as hard as they could. The sun was already painting colors low in the sky. Will needed to get home before dinner or his mother would be worried, and then really angry when he showed up, because she had been so worried.

Alex had twisted his ankle, Ben had scraped his leg on a large stick that somehow found its way into the "ring," and Will had bent his left pinkie so far back he couldn't feel it anymore. He was going to pay the price for that for a while. Hopefully, it would heal before basketball tryouts. But he felt most like an idiot for asking Claire to join him and then ignoring her completely.

"She'll get over it," Ben told Will. When they heard a car behind them, they fell back into a single line until it passed.

"You know Claire, she's not a girly girl. She's fine," Alex shouted up ahead.

"We should have just stopped," Will said, mostly telling himself.

Ben sped up beside him. "You like her, don't you?"

Will didn't need to answer.

"Hey, man. I'm sorry," Alex said, dropping back on the other side.

Ben and Alex got home first, and Will rode the last quarter mile by himself. He could see the lights on in his kitchen window. His mom was probably making dinner. The girls were probably watching TV or taking a bath. It wasn't so different, really, than it had ever been. Will's dad had sometimes been home for only five or six nights a month anyway.

And yet everything was different.

Will came to a stop at the end of his driveway. He looked up. It wasn't dark yet, but the sky had that hint of fall, of night coming early and taking the day away. If he got back on his bike now, he could be at Claire's house in three minutes. And home again before dinner.

He had no idea what he was going to do or say, or even if trying to talk to Claire was the right thing to do. He knew only that he had to do something, because doing nothing would feel worse.

When he turned ten, Will had had a real party at the bowling alley over in Somerset. It was one of the few times his dad was going to be around on his actual birthday, and besides, hitting that two-digit number was a big deal, wasn't it?

"Of course I'll be there."

But that year was also the year that kids in his grade had started shifting into separate categories, some willingly and others not so willingly. There was smart and not so smart. Higher math groups and lower reading levels. Popular girls and the girls that sat alone. Boys that could throw a ball, and boys that constantly got beaned in the head with the volleyball no matter how hard they tried to return the volley. In a class so small, it just looked all the more obvious who was who.

"I don't know what to do about my birthday," Will told his dad.

"About that boy from school?"

"Yeah. I don't really want him to come to my party."

They were picking up sticks from the front lawn, sticks and branches that had fallen in the last rainstorm. When Will's dad was home, he wanted to do as many chores and repairs around the house as he could. Will always tagged along and helped.

"Then don't invite him."

"But he'll have his feelings hurt." Will threw one long branch into the woods behind their house and followed after his dad. "And we were okay friends last year."

"Then invite him."

"But I don't really want him to be there. He'll ruin everything. He's gotten so weird, and loud about it too."

"Well, you've got to make a decision."

"But how?"

Will's dad was holding a bundle of wood and leaves in his arms. He looked like a tree himself, tall and strong, like nothing could ever hurt him. He knew everything.

"Jump ahead in time and ask yourself how you will feel if you don't invite him."

So Will closed his eyes. And he could imagine his party, everything going so well, all the presents he would get, the hot dogs and ice-cream cake, and then everyone would go home and it would have been a perfect day.

"Okay," Will said. "I did. Great party."

His dad went on, "And then how are you going to

feel when you see this boy in your class the next day?"

Will closed his eyes again.

He would go back to school, and this kid would be the only one from his class that wasn't talking about it. Maybe everyone else would be talking about their bowling scores or asking Will if he liked their gifts. Or just raving about how much fun they'd had at his party. Everyone but that one kid. Just imagining that felt pretty bad already.

"So I have to decide by what will make me feel *worse*?" Will asked his dad. "Not what will make me feel *better*?"

His dad dumped his armload of branches onto a pile behind the shed. "It's not about what makes you feel better or worse. If it's the right thing to do and you know it, you should do it."

"Even if my party sucks?" Will said, but he knew the answer.

9/11

September 11, 2001
7:15 a.m. EDT
Columbus, Ohio

Two years ago Naheed had come home from elementary school and announced she was going to be a heart surgeon when she grew up. In health class they had done a unit on body systems, bones, nerves, and organs.

And on the circulatory system. And the heart.

The heart was the center of everything, pumping blood to everywhere in the body, carrying oxygen to all vital parts, including the brain. Naheed wanted to be the one who fixed the heart.

"Why a surgeon?" her father asked. He was a neurologist; her mother, a pediatrician.

"Because I'm good with my hands." Naheed held up all ten fingers, as if seeing them would be explanation enough.

Her parents laughed, but Naheed could tell they were pleased, and science became her favorite subject. Until yesterday, that is, and today Naheed didn't even want to go to school.

"Naheed, you look tired. Are you tired? Don't you feel well?" Naheed's mother put her hand to Naheed's forehead. "You don't feel warm."

"I'm not warm," Naheed said. "I just didn't sleep well."

"Oh no, that's our fault," Aunt Judith said. She was sitting at the kitchen table drinking coffee. "Uncle and I are so sorry. But don't worry, you girls will get your rooms back this afternoon."

Nouri jumped up from her seat and into Aunt Judith's lap. "Oh no, you're leaving? I don't want you to leave."

Nouri always knew just what to say, because she meant it. She would never have gotten herself into this jam. Nouri would have been happy explaining to Eliza what her head covering was and why she wore it. And that would have been the end of that.

But then again, to be fair, Nouri wasn't in middle school yet.

"Oh, you are such a sweetie," Aunt Judith said, hugging Nouri. "Yes, we have a flight back this afternoon.

So we all need to say good-bye this morning before you leave for school."

At the mention of the word "school," Naheed must have groaned out loud, at which point Nouri felt the need to share with Aunt Judith an account of the two boys who had been teasing her older sister. And it all happened just as their father was coming down for breakfast, followed by Uncle Iman.

"What is this?" Uncle Iman asked. "Who was harassing my niece about her hijab?" He took up a lot of room in the kitchen, and it wasn't because of his size.

"No one," Naheed said quickly. She shot a warning look to her sister.

"Well, is this true?" Naheed's father asked.

"She can handle it, *eshgham*. We talked about it last night," Naheed's mother broke in. She poured both men their coffee.

"But you didn't tell your father," Uncle Iman said.

"There was nothing to tell," Naheed went on, but she was beginning to see her story growing wings and feathers and flying away, too far for her ever to catch again. "I will take care of it today. And if I can't, I promise I will tell you, Baba."

Naheed's father looked at his brother and then at his watch. "Well, I have to make rounds this morning.

September 11, 2001
8:07 a.m. EDT
Shanksville, Pennsylvania

"Remember my birthday party in third grade?" Will was asking his mother.

"Not exactly, why?"

"Because it sucked."

Will's mother laughed, which was good to hear. She didn't laugh like she used to, and Will liked being able to make his mother even a little happy.

She was rushing around in her usual morning ritual, making breakfast and lunch, putting on her eye makeup while looking at her reflection in the toaster oven. His sisters were still upstairs.

Last night going over to Claire's house had been a bust. What had he been thinking?

The problem was he hadn't had a plan, not really. Just

the idea that he would try to explain to Claire something he couldn't understand himself: why he had acted like such a jerk.

When he got to her house, he realized he probably needed a little something more than that. He stood thinking for a serious half a minute or so. It didn't seem likely that knocking on her front door and possibly seeing her mom or dad, or even her older brother, was the right move.

He had seen old movies where the guy stood on the lawn and threw little pebbles at the girl's bedroom window, and that did seem kind of romantic, especially if Claire had seen the same movies. But Will didn't know which window was Claire's, which made him think those old movies were really misleading and probably shouldn't be shown on television.

Maybe he would spot her up there on the second floor. Then, as luck would have it, and Will sure needed some, Claire walked right out her front door.

"What are you doing here?" She was surprised, if not anything better, like happy to see him.

"Nothing." This seemed to be Will's go-to response lately, and that definitely wasn't going to work in this case. "I mean," Will said, "I came to apologize."

Claire looked at him, and for a tiny second something close to a smile nearly moved across her eyes and mouth.

Not a bad move, Will was about to congratulate himself. Nothing like a sincere apology. Girls liked that. Except maybe he looked a little too smug a little too soon.

"Forget it, Will," Claire threw back. "You don't have to apologize. You didn't do anything wrong. Go back and play with your friends. Next time just don't ask me to be your cheering section, okay?"

"I didn't—"

"I've got better things to do." Claire stepped down onto the grass, as if Will had already left, and started calling for her cat.

"Here, kitty. Here, kitty, kitty."

"You're looking for your cat?" Will asked.

She didn't answer.

This was not going well.

"Why do you want him inside? It's so nice out," Will tried. "I think it's going to be warm tonight."

Girls loved their cats, right? And talking about the weather seemed pretty safe.

"Because there are coyotes and bobcats, and I'd really like my cat *not* to be eaten this evening, if it's all the same to you."

"Can I help you look, at least?"

Claire shrugged.

They found the cat, but neither the potential conversation nor the afternoon was redeemed. He said he was sorry again, Claire went inside, and Will rode home.

"Does this have something to do with your late-night excursion?" Will's mother asked. She dropped sandwiches into the girls' lunch boxes.

"It was six thirty, Mom. Not exactly late-night."

And she laughed again. Twice in one morning might have been a record for the year. "Well, does it?" she asked.

"Kinda."

"Wanna tell me about it?"

"No."

His mother looked at him thoughtfully. "There are some things you really need your dad for, don't you?"

She hadn't ever talked like that before. Just stating it out loud, acknowledging what the loss of his father meant to Will.

Will felt bad, worse than he had a second ago, but it also felt good, in a way, to have someone else who understood how bad he felt. And all of a sudden Will felt like crying, the way that kind of sorrow would swoop in and punch him in the gut. He was almost used to it.

He could use his dad's advice right now. If not his advice, just his presence.

Will felt like crying, but he didn't. It passed, more quickly than it might have a year ago, or even six months. Instead he asked his mom, "Are you mad at Dad?"

"For dying like that?" she asked.

Will nodded.

"Well, yeah. I was. I still am, sometimes. But I understand, and I love him for the man he was. The man he'll always be. That was your dad. He couldn't be any other way. He would never walk away from something. He'd never let someone else's hands get dirty but not his."

Will's mom sat down at the kitchen table with her son. "I know you're angry. I get why. I don't want to talk you out of it, but I want you to understand."

"I understand. I'm not dumb," Will said. He kept his eyes down on his hands, his hands down on the table. "I know he did a good thing. He tried to help someone. But I just wish—"

"I do too."

"And then I get mad at that other man, for having a stroke or whatever he had, like he shouldn't have been driving, but then I know that doesn't make sense either."

Will knew his mom wanted to hug him, put her arms around him and take him on her lap, and make everything all better, the way she could when he was little. He was really glad she didn't try.

"But it was the wrong thing to do, wasn't it? Dad getting out of his rig on the highway that way," Will went on. "If he could do it again, he wouldn't do that."

Will's mother shrugged. Her shoulders were trembling, but she continued. She was stronger than she looked. "Your dad wasn't one to regret things, but yes, I'm sure he would do it differently." She wiped her eyes and stood up. "You'd better hurry if you want to catch the bus."

"I might just ride my bike today, if that's okay."

His mother smiled. "It's okay."

September 11, 2001
5:30 a.m. PDT
Los Angeles, California

On the other end, three thousand miles away in New York City, a phone was ringing and ringing but no one was answering.

C'mon. C'mon. Pick up, Mom. Pick up.

Aimee had set her alarm so she could reach her mom before her mom called her, before her mom left for her meeting. She wanted to tell her everything. Tell her about her first day. About how she met one nice girl and one mean one. About gym class—*You wouldn't believe what the gym teacher's name is*—and about math, and lunch period. She would have to bring a snack from now on, she would inform her mom.

She wanted to say she was sorry.

She was sorry for being rude on the phone and

pretending she couldn't hear her mom. She was sorry she'd had a horrible, horrible, horrible day, but she shouldn't have taken it out on her mother. She wanted to tell her mom how much she just missed her. And couldn't wait for her to get back.

Though she might not want to share how she had thought her mom and dad were getting divorced, even if all that had been cleared up last night at the restaurant.

It was a weekday, Monday, but Aimee's dad had wanted to take her out to a nice dinner. Aimee glanced across the menu to the prices as she was picking what she might want to eat. It was expensive.

She ran her fingers over the real tablecloth and noticed the napkins were cloth too. "Why did we come to such a fancy place?" Aimee asked her dad from across the table.

"What? This place?" her dad joked. "Well, for my special little girl, why not?"

Suddenly Aimee felt sick.

Was this going to be the big announcement? Were her parents getting a divorce? Was that why they were here at this expensive restaurant?

That's how it always happens in the movies, the dad and his daughter, the china plates, the shiny glasses of water, maybe even a Shirley Temple with a too-red cherry, and then he breaks the bad news.

"But what about Mom? Isn't Mom your special girl?" Aimee blanched. Her insides wrenched up into a knot.

Aimee's father looked at her. He tipped his head and sort of crinkled his brow. "What's this all about, honey? What's wrong?"

Aimee felt tears burning behind her eyes and that sharp, knifelike twinge in her throat that always signaled a flood of tears. But she held them back. There was so much. There was too much. At the same time she didn't want to go back to school tomorrow without knowing. She needed to know the truth about her parents once and for all.

"Are you and Mom splitting up?" Aimee heard herself asking.

Her father dropped his menu. It clattered on his plate. He looked hard at Aimee. "No, Aimee. Not at all. Why would you even ask that?"

So Aimee told her dad about her first day of school, Vanessa, Bridget, Tom Cruise, and Ryan Phillippe. She had never heard her father laugh so hard. In public.

"I'm sorry, Aimee." Her dad composed himself. "I don't mean to make light of it. But no, your mom and I are not getting divorced. We love each other very much and we love you."

Boy, did *that* sound suspicious. Her dad must have read her face.

"Seriously, Aimee. Stop it," he told her. "You're just going to have to believe me. Your mother and I have never talked about it. Never. Not once."

Aimee took a big drink of water. "Then who's Chris?" she asked.

"Chris?" her dad said. "From your mom's office? Chris Weissman? She's your mom's new boss. Why?"

"She?"

"She."

When her appetite returned, Aimee was able to eat everything she had ordered; salad, steak, french fries, and dessert. She ate like she hadn't eaten in days, when in fact she hadn't eaten in one whole day. Food never tastes as good as when you are really hungry.

It was pitch black at five thirty in the morning in Los Angeles, but the sun would be up in Manhattan. Her mother would be getting ready for her big meeting at the whatever-it-was building. She would be all dressed in her gray suit and black high heels—which Aimee had put her stamp of approval on—maybe putting on another coat of mascara. She might even be making her bed in the hotel. Aimee smiled. Her mom was like that.

Aimee held the phone in her hand, sitting up in bed, and listened to the ringing.

C'mon, Mom. C'mon. Pick up already.

Please. Please. Please.

I miss you so much, Mom.

Just pick up.

September 11, 2001
8:14 a.m. EDT
Brooklyn, New York

An unexcused absence meant detention, but for some reason the principal decided to give Sergio a second chance. Possibly Sergio was still riding the wave of his math award, giving the school a good name. Or maybe it was because everyone deserves a second chance.

The principal had called him into her office first thing that morning. "But, Sergio, next time . . ."

She sat across from him, behind a desk piled with papers and envelopes, files—apparently, she had a lot of work to do. Still, she was nice about the whole thing. "Next time I can't cut you any slack. Don't miss school again, Sergio. I don't have to tell you, showing up already puts you ahead of the rest."

"Yes, ma'am." Sergio nodded. "I won't. I will. I mean, I know."

"Okay, then get to class. Oh, and Sergio . . ." She stopped him just as he got to the door to her office. "I hope whatever you had to do yesterday without your grandmother's permission was well worth it. I hope it wasn't any kind of trouble. If you are in any kind of trouble, you know you can come and talk to me."

"I know that," Sergio said.

It wasn't trouble, and it *had* been worth it, spending the day with Gideon. Sergio thought about yesterday all the way down the hall.

He was even wearing one of the new T-shirts Gideon had bought for him. Gideon had said it was payment for saving that guy's life and it was the least he could do. And then he offered to take Sergio to lunch.

They had sat across from each other in a booth at the diner. Sergio's grandmother hadn't been happy about the call from Gideon's cell phone. She wasn't happy Sergio had missed school, but whatever Gideon told her must have meant something. When Sergio got on the line, she was calmer. She said she wasn't going to cover for him at school, but she wouldn't punish him either. And he just had to be back home by dinner.

"I didn't do anything," Sergio said. "And I doubt that guy would have died, anyway."

"He probably had a hemorrhage, a bleed in his brain you couldn't see," Gideon said. "He might have died. You wouldn't believe some of the things I've seen. Last year we pulled a young girl from a car after an accident up on the West Side Highway. She had lost control and hit a pole and then a wall—barely any damage to the car. Or to her. She hit her head in just the wrong way, I guess. She looked like she was sleeping."

"But she wasn't?"

"She wasn't." Gideon shook his head from side to side, slowly, as if he was feeling it all over again.

Sergio had ordered a chocolate milk shake. Gideon, vanilla. And they had just talked.

"Who gets the chocolate? I'm guessing your son?" the waitress said. She stood at their booth holding up two large canisters, both dripping with condensation from the cold ice cream inside.

Gideon looked at Sergio. "He's not my dad," Sergio said. "But, yeah. The chocolate is mine."

"Well, you two look alike." She set the shakes down.

They did, in a way. Maybe in that way white people think black people all look similar. But then again, they both poured their shakes into their respective glasses and then lifted the metal canisters to their mouths, drinking down the leftovers first. And then again, there was a kind of facial likeness between them, a shade of skin color. Sergio found himself looking at Gideon, watching him. Listening. When he looked down at his own hand, he saw his fist clenched, like it always was, and he let it unfurl.

Gideon wanted to know about the math award. He seemed interested and impressed.

"You could do anything," Gideon told him. "Anything you want with your life."

"Maybe I want to be a fireman." Sergio bit into his burger.

"Fireman, huh? You could do that," Gideon said. "I'd be proud to work next to you one day."

"Or a doctor."

Gideon nodded, like he didn't think that was strange at all.

Now, sitting in class, Sergio looked up at the clock over the door, at the white face, at the black minute hand, which moved unbelievably slowly, until another sixty seconds had gone by, it clicked into its place, locked, and the first school bell rang out.

Six hours more and he'd be free again for the day. It

was 8:44 exactly, and Sergio knew where he would be going right after school. He could look out the window and see Lower Manhattan, the financial district, where he knew Gideon's station house was.

Gideon had told him to come by anytime to the firehouse. If they weren't on a call, all the guys would be there. Sergio could even hang out. Gideon would introduce him around. Show him the station.

"If it's okay with your grandma," Gideon said. "I've always wanted a little brother. Oh, and hey, if it's okay with you."

Sergio was already dreaming about it. He barely listened as his teacher droned on about something. For the first time in a long time, he felt a kind of eagerness for the day ahead.

One hundred and twenty seconds clicked by. Flight 11, a commercial airliner carrying eighty-one passengers and eleven crew members, which had been hijacked shortly after taking off from Boston's Logan International Airport, flew directly into the North Tower of the World Trade Center and exploded.

Someone standing at the window started rambling about a dark mushroom of smoke rising from across the river, and the bell, without any awareness of what was going on, rang for first period.

September 11, 2001
8:54 a.m. EDT
Columbus, Ohio

Flight 77—with fifty-eight passengers and six crew members on board—on its way to Los Angeles International Airport, deviated from its course, turning south directly over Ohio, where, thirty-five thousand feet below, Naheed was sitting in language arts class, listening to Virginia Whitworth give her book report on *The Outsiders*.

"Oh, I read that book," Naheed whispered to no one in particular. "I loved it."

But then Naheed hardly heard the rest of Virginia's report. She was working out in her mind what she was going to say to Eliza and how she could make things better. Instinctually she reached up to pull down her headband and adjust her veil. It was her thinking cap.

Naheed knew she'd never get everyone to stop teasing Eliza, but she herself could be nicer. She could be a friend to her, and maybe that would help. It was the right thing to do, and the truth was, nobody was going to stop being Naheed's friend just because she was Eliza's friend.

She hoped.

The bell rang as Virginia was finishing, but the teacher made everyone wait until she had given the homework for tomorrow, which meant they all had twenty-five seconds less time to get to their next class.

Today was Tuesday and it was B week, which meant a double period of science. Which meant Naheed could start implementing her making-amends plan right away. Eliza would be in class. Today, Naheed had taken her science book with her so she would be on time.

But when she got there, nothing looked right.

A bunch of kids were bouncing around, some were standing at the back of the room, but no one was sitting down. It was like the lunchroom on a Friday afternoon before school vacation when the cafeteria monitors weren't paying attention.

In the far corner the television was on, and Mrs. Salinger was staring at it, with her back to the classroom. Sure, sometimes they watched videos in science, but today they were supposed to continue working on their theories and experiments. And since when did Mrs. Salinger let things get so out of control? She didn't even turn around to yell at the boys who were playing with the Bunsen burners.

Eliza was standing at their desk, facing the wrong way, toward the back of the room, not moving. Naheed had never seen her so still and so quiet.

A few more kids went to stand next to Mrs. Salinger and stare at the TV, but Mrs. Salinger didn't seem to notice anything but the screen. This wasn't like her at all. It looked as if the television was turned to a news channel. The CNN "live" logo was stamped across the bottom, but that was all Naheed could see. She always hated the news. Why was everyone watching it? And why were they so quiet about it?

But now was as good a time as any to talk to Eliza, with all this freedom. With nobody paying attention.

"Hey, Eliza, can I talk to you a minute?" Naheed started. She might not get another chance.

"Something terrible has happened," Eliza said. She looked upset, but then again, Eliza got frantic if her pencils weren't lined up.

"I know," Naheed said. "And about that—I am so sorry. So why don't I make it up to you, and you sit with me, with us, at lunch today?"

Eliza took her eyes away from the television. "Really?" Her face brightened.

Naheed nodded.

Hey, that was easy. And it actually felt good. "Really," she said.

"Okay, that's enough. Everyone back to their seats," Mrs. Salinger suddenly yelled out.

Naheed looked around the room. Mrs. Salinger had turned off the television, but the kids who had been watching didn't move. Something was wrong. Maybe that's what Eliza had meant when she said something terrible had happened. She had been watching the news.

Now Naheed felt silly, but when she turned to ask Eliza what had happened, Mrs. Salinger preempted her.

"No more talking," she ordered. "Take out your work. This has nothing to do with us."

What didn't?

Mrs. Salinger repeated it, as if trying to convince herself. "This has nothing to do with us."

September 11, 2001
5:31 a.m. PDT
Los Angeles, California

The phone rang so many times, Aimee was amazed her call hadn't gone to voice mail yet. "Hello? Hello?" She thought she heard the connection click. Someone answered, but there was a lot of noisy interference.

"Mom?" Aimee said.

Her bedroom was dark and she whispered quietly, as if she might wake up her sleeping stuffed animals, each one from another time in her life, when things were less confusing. Barney the purple dinosaur had been given to her by her grandpa Jerry. The giant, soft rabbit, missing a nose, she had had since she was a baby. She didn't even know the woman who had given it to her when she was born, an old college friend of her mom's. There was a smiling Bart Simpson doll, with a hard plastic head and soft arms and legs. She had gotten that from her dad when she was in second grade. She had never watched the show, but she loved that doll. Bears and camels and an imaginary creature sewn from patchwork scraps, all holders of hugs and kisses, friends and family soaked into the fabric, the fur, and the stuffing.

The ringing had stopped, and the static coming from the other end got louder.

"Mom? Are you there?"

Aimee looked at the clock radio glowing next to her bed: 5:31 in the morning. It would be 8:31 in New York. Her mother's meeting would be starting soon. She'd be frazzled and rushed and she wouldn't be able to listen. But if Aimee could just get a word out. If they could connect for one second.

"Mom?"

Static.

And then, "Aimee? Aimee, what are you doing up so early? Is everything all right?"

Relief washed over her body, hearing her mother's voice coming across a whole continent and three time zones right into Aimee's bedroom. Everything was going to be all right.

"Hey, Mom. I'm fine. I'm just sorry about yesterday.

I didn't mean to hang up and be so rude. I'm sorry, but I just wanted to—"

"Oh, Aimee, I'm . . . mad. I'm just . . . there. I know there's something . . . on. And I want you to tell me all about it when I . . . I . . . you've been hurting and I haven't been there."

Almost every other word was lost, and then there was static again.

"Mom, I can't hear you."

"Can you hear me now?"

"Mom, it's just that—"

"But, sweetie, I'm running so late this morning. I'm supposed to be downtown by nine, and I haven't even left the hotel yet."

"Mom, I just want to ask you a question. One thing."

"I . . . ten minutes to . . . Trade Center and up to their offices. Oh, what floor are they on again? My car service . . . come . . . morning. We . . . to grab a cab."

Aimee could hear her mother's voice a little better now, against the sounds of New York City streets, horns blaring, and sirens rising in pitch and zooming away, but it was clear her mom couldn't hear her at all.

"Sweet . . . I'll call you when I'm . . . I promise. Taxi!"

"Mom . . . but, Mom . . ." She gave up trying to shout into the phone. Her mom was so far away. It wasn't only the miles, it was everything that had come between them. Aimee started to cry. Again, just like last night.

"Aimee?"

All Aimee could manage was to sob. Once she had started crying, she couldn't stop. Her mother couldn't hear her.

A man's voice broke through the buzzing. "Sure, lady. Where to?"

"Never mind," Aimee's mom was saying to someone. "Sorry. What? Yes, oh sure, you take the cab. I need to talk to my daughter. Yes, I'm sure. I'll meet you back at the hotel later."

Aimee heard a car door slam. The reception was better. The static suddenly lifted. Her mother's voice was clear.

"Now, talk to me, Aimee. I'm going to go back in the lobby and sit down. Can you hear me?"

"Yes, but . . ." Aimee sniffed hard and gulped it down. "But what about your meeting?"

"I'll make something up. They can do without me," her mom said. "But you, my Aimeleh, I can't do without you."

September 11, 2001
9:53 a.m. EDT
Brooklyn, New York

When a second plane, Flight 175, with fifty-six passengers and nine crew members on board, flew directly into the South Tower of the World Trade Center, there was no mistaking what was happening, and nothing was going to keep the older kids in school. Flames were leaping from the two towers now, reaching into the blue sky. Gray smoke formed a giant cloud that hung over the buildings and expanded outward like paint slowly being spilled onto an empty canvas.

Sergio could hear sirens coming from all directions, wailing and screaming out, and he thought immediately of the firemen. It was an old and far away, but very familiar, feeling of loss that leaped into his gut. The kind of feeling that had no words, that his body had held on to even if his memory had not.

Gideon would be running toward the fire, running to help. Heading directly toward that mess. Running right into it.

"That's what we're trained to do," he had told Sergio just yesterday.

Sergio stood at the window of his classroom with the rest of the kids, hoping to see what was going on. He didn't want to feel this dread that was building up inside him. He didn't want to be scared, but he was.

He could remember Gideon's face, his expression, his calm but commanding voice in the subway. How did he do that? How did he stay so focused with all the mess going on around him?

Sergio turned away from the window. The teacher hadn't shown up yet. Maybe she wasn't coming. Maybe he should be going somewhere, like everyone else in the halls.

Did Gideon have no fear, or did he just push it away?

There was fear in the classroom now. It fed off itself, from one body to another, like heat shimmering off asphalt in the summer, undefined and blurry. No one knew what was happening, but somehow everyone now knew it was something bad. Really bad.

The halls were filled with kids and teachers. Parents

were starting to show up, running through the building, grabbing their children. Crying.

Grown-ups were crying.

Then the principal came over the loudspeaker, dismissing all the upper grades and telling everyone to go directly to their homes.

Girls were crying in the halls. Boys were too. Their voices carried into the classroom.

A plane had accidentally hit one of the Twin Towers. Accidentally? And then another one. *Accidentally?*

Some kids said they had seen it happen.

"It was a bomb."

"It's an attack."

"It was a plane."

"It flew directly into the side of the building. That's no accident."

Sergio walked over and turned on the television in the back of the classroom. He started flipping through every station. Or was someone else doing that, and he was just standing, just watching the screen? It didn't matter. He struggled to stay inside his body. To focus and push away the fear.

One of the TV reporters said there were giant, gaping holes in the sides of the Twin Towers, like a cartoon explosion. Someone else said it was the end of the world.

Fear was like a cloud itself, threatening to suffocate him.

Within minutes, it seemed—an hour, it seemed too—the school started to empty out; classroom doors flung open, glass windows cracking. The world was on fire, fierce yellow and angry red. The sky over Manhattan was gray with soot in a halo of blue and a shroud of black.

Fifty-six minutes after the second plane crashed, with only a few kids—Sergio being one of them—still left in the classroom staring out the window, there was a horrible, cracking, popping *bang-bang-bang-bang* booming sound that lasted forever. He could hear it in his head, and like a crack in the fourth dimension, a fracture of the Euclidean plane, Sergio could watch it happening on the television.

"Oh no. It's going down. The whole building. It's going down!"

Someone in the room started counting the seconds, as if no explosion could last that long.

It couldn't, but it did.

"Seven. Eight. Nine. Ten."

Cracking. Popping. Exploding. *Bang, bang, bang*, as if each floor was falling onto the other, and when it finally ended, there was nothing but smoke. No red. No yellow.

"I'm getting out of here."

"Holy crap, that's it for me."

There were no thoughts left to think. Sergio's body followed the rest of students into the chaos.

Everyone started pouring out into the streets, some running away, and some headed, like lemmings to the sea, toward the waterfront. Running toward the river, trying to get a better look. Kids were climbing fences and scaling fire escapes of strangers' houses, just to see what they could see. And from all angles, from in front and behind, came the wailing sound of sirens. First responders, Gideon had called them—the firefighters and police that arrived first on a scene and took care of the wounded.

"We are the ones who have more training in medical emergencies," Gideon had explained. "Not as much as EMTs, but more than your average first-aid course. You know what I mean?"

Sergio had nodded. "Like you did with that guy on the train."

"Exactly."

It was clear that the world was about to blow apart, if it hadn't already, and suddenly nothing else mattered but getting home. It was a primitive instinct, a drive, a need to find family no matter how far.

Get home.

Sergio started to make his way back to his apartment.

His grandmother would be at work by now. So should he turn and head that way?

Or would she be making her way to him? Would she be running home too?

Home. He knew he should run home, and he listened to his footsteps hitting the sidewalk pavement, loud thumping, one after the other, in rhythm with his breathing, like he was inside of a wind tunnel. All sounds were exaggerated. The world was screaming out loud.

Ambulances sped by on the street, one after another after another. His grandmother had taught him to pray, but he had long since stopped doing that when she wasn't around. What good was it? But there was too much noise. Too much panic and fear, spilling into the streets and rising up into the sky. Sergio ran and he prayed.

For his grandmother to be home when he got there.

For himself to know what to do. And for Gideon to be safe.

Police sirens were wailing, and cops were not paying one bit of attention to all the black teenagers loitering outside the school, running down the sidewalks and the middle of the street.

Fire trucks.

And more fire trucks, all speeding toward the bridge in a blur of red and white, a deafening, endless ribbon.

Heading toward the bridge, heading directly into the chaos, the flames and sirens and smoke. Gideon was heading right into it. Sergio was running the other way.

But what else could he do?

Get home and hope that home was still there.

There were a few boys from his school leaning over a metal fence and straining their necks.

Sergio called up, "What do you see?"

"Oh, God," one of the boys kept saying, and nothing more. Nothing else. "Oh, God."

Sergio felt his feet leave the ground. He hoisted himself up. He gripped the metal bar at the top of the fence.

"Hey, make room."

The boys scrambled over, and Sergio positioned himself as high on the fence as he could. From this vantage point it was a clear view, directly across the river to where the World Trade Center had once stood. Sergio could see people, hundreds of people, streaming off the island of Manhattan, and they were all white.

Even the black folks were white. White like powder. White like ghosts. Running in slow motion. Walking across the bridge into Brooklyn. White with the ashes of a thousand dead covering their faces, their bodies. Covering the earth.

September 11, 2001
9:41 a.m. EDT
Shanksville, Pennsylvania

Will knew he would have to ride by Claire's house on his way to school, which was most likely the reason he veered his bike to the side and took a little rest, hoping that by the time he got back on, she would be long gone. Then he wouldn't have to face her. Not just yet. In fact, skipping school entirely seemed like it might not be a bad idea. For that reason, and for the fact that this day was probably the most perfect day Will could ever remember, even if he had ruined what might possibly have been his only chance at being with a girl that he really, really liked.

Will lay faceup in the grass, his hands folded under his head. There wasn't a cloud in the sky to dream about or make up stories about, but Will dreamed anyway. And as he often did, he imagined that his dad was still alive, that it had all been some horrible mistake, a mix-up in the hospital, mistaken identity. His dad would come home one afternoon after a really long, long haul gig, and he'd wonder what all the hubbub was about.

Wouldn't that be funny?

No, that's why they had had the funeral. The dark suit. The service and the burial. All those people and all that food. Will shook his head back and forth in the grass, shaking the thoughts out of his mind. Because there had to be something more than either the fantasy or horror.

There had to be, and there was.

Will closed his eyes and let himself just remember his dad: his dad throwing him across his parents' king-size bed, pretending to wrestle, doing a Jerry Lawler pile driver and then a Sgt. Slaughter cobra clutch. Then his father would pretend to get tired, or pretend to make a bad choice, leaving his arms exposed or his back wide open, and Will would bounce across the mattress, acting out a Randy Savage elbow drop off the top rope, and take his father all the way down, where his dad would flop around and beg for mercy.

For the longest time, for years after he should have known better, Will really believed he had won.

Sort of.

A smile grew across his face as the warm memory took hold in his mind and then his whole body. Until Will felt the heat of the sun disappear and he heard a voice directly over his head. "What's up, there, William Rittenhouse?"

That was Claire.

Will jumped to his feet, and his sneakers got tangled under him for a long second, but he made a swift, semi-graceful recovery and stood upright.

"What are *you* doing here? How did you find me?"

She pointed back toward the road. "I recognized your bike."

"Oh." It took Will a little while to put it together. "But why aren't you in school?"

"I decided I needed a personal day." Claire smiled conspiratorially. "So I told my mom I wasn't feeling well, and when she went to work—well, it was so beautiful out, you know what I mean? And then I saw your bike there." She waited a beat and added, "I was hoping I'd see you."

"Me?"

Without saying so, they both starting walking back toward the road. They picked up their bikes, but neither one of them got on.

"We're probably both going to get in trouble," Will said, pushing his bike forward.

"Well, you will for sure." She laughed.

Will knew this was exactly what he had hoped would happen yesterday when he asked Claire to ride bikes after school. Almost twenty-four hours and a couple of embarrassing moments later, but here they were. It was hard not to feel excited, excited but calm. Calm but happy. It felt right.

"I'm sorry I was so mean to you last night," Claire said.

They rolled their bikes over the gravel, not in any hurry.

"It's okay. I deserved it."

"No, you didn't," Claire said. "You were just fooling around with your friends. I guess I just . . ."

He didn't want her to feel sorry for him. He didn't want her to like him because his father had died and she thought he was fragile. He wanted her to like him.

"I guess I . . . ," Claire went on. "I guess I just like you, that's all."

Claire took Will's hand, and they walked that way for a long while without saying anything. Will wanted to reach out and stop their bikes from rolling. He wanted to lean over and press his lips against Claire's, because he knew hers would be soft, and warm, and that it would be perfect. Like the crystalline blue sky over their heads, and the gentle wind that cooled them, and the expanse of green lawns that he had known all his life.

And it was.

Just like that.

When he kissed her.

Neither one of them heard the discordant sound of a jet engine coming near until it roared right above their heads. Then a huge flash of silver reflected in the sun. They both looked up to see a plane flying on its side, so near, so close to the tops of the trees, that later both Will and Claire would mention being able to see the metal rivets on the wings. And then it was gone.

A few seconds later, at 10:03 a.m., the plane hit something so violently and with such force it shook the ground. Windows, wide open to the spectacularly beautiful fall day, would slam shut in homes along Lambertsville Road and as far away as the high school. Tiles in the ceiling of the elementary school would shift like they were made of paper, and for weeks after, debris would be discovered scattered across nearby backyards, roped off with yellow police tape.

Flight 93, with thirty-seven passengers and seven crew members on board, had left Newark forty minutes late because of runway congestion. That gap of time might have allowed friends and family on the ground, who had been watching the horrifying news from New York and Washington, DC, to warn those on the plane of what was most likely, though unfathomably, about to happen. It was not, however, enough time to prevent the course of events, only to alter them; which the passengers and crew did bravely, even though it cost them all their lives.

The plane dug a trench more than thirty feet deep into the spongy earth of the old strip cuts on Skyline Drive, directly between two hushed, abandoned pieces of mining equipment. It scorched the pine trees standing by in witness. It sent a plume of dark smoke up into the sky, charcoal black into the robin's-egg blue of the once most perfect day.

September 11, 2001
10:45 a.m. EDT
Columbus, Ohio

What was happening?

Why?

Parents had started showing up to get their kids and take them home. Just a few at first, then a few more. One girl from Mrs. Salinger's class got called down to the office, and another mom showed up right at the classroom door. She looked like she had been crying. She asked for her daughter, and they were gone. Something bad had happened in New York City, but why everyone was so upset, no one could really say. None of the teachers were interested in teaching anything, and after a while it felt oddly like a snow day, an in-school snow day on the warmest, clearest, most beautiful day of the year. Naheed moved from one period to the next with the rest of her classmates, who were mostly undisturbed, and mostly glad not to be taking tests or giving reports or whatever they had thought they were going to be doing that morning. No one was explaining what was going on until an announcement came over the PA that there was to be an entire-sixth-grade assembly in the library in five minutes. Seventh graders were to report to the auditorium. Eighth graders to the cafeteria.

Immediately.

"Did you hear anything?" Tommy came up next to Naheed as they were making their way down the hall toward the library.

"I'm not sure," Naheed said.

"I think it's about a bomb in New York City," Tommy said.

"It was a plane." Another boy from their grade came up beside them. "Mr. Nemerofsky let us have the radio on in math class," he said. "It was a huge plane, and it was on purpose."

"That's a lie," Tommy said. "That's not true."

"Oh, yeah?" The boy kept walking forward but looked back over his shoulder at them. "Then why do you think we're having this big assembly? Just to hear about some random accident a thousand miles from here?" He nearly bumped into the line of kids waiting to file into the library.

"It wasn't New York. It was Washington, DC," another girl told them.

Either way it was far away from here.

At least they got out of class. And they were all standing here doing nothing, which was certainly better than having to go to PE.

The nearly two hundred sixth graders poured into the library, and the teachers shouted out directions:

"Blue group sits here."

"Fill in these spots up front."

"Everyone on the floor."

"No pushing."

"Sit still."

"And be quiet."

Kids were talking, shifting around, and slowly making their way to the carpet. At the far end, by the library office, a couple of boys were balling up paper and lobbing it over onto other boys' heads, then ducking down and laughing. Nothing seemed out of the ordinary or too serious.

Just a snow day in September, right?

Naheed wanted to find Eliza. This would be a nice time to be nice. To sit with her and let Eliza know she was serious about being her friend. But there were so many people. It was hard to make out any one particular person.

Naheed was scanning the room for Eliza, but she began to notice the teachers standing around the outside of the circle of students, their expressions solemn. They weren't chatting with one another or looking for unruly boys. They were preoccupied, as they had been all morning, waiting for the principal to start talking.

"Sit down, now!" It was Mrs. Salinger. Her face was strange. Her makeup was smeared and it looked like scary Halloween paint. "Everyone sit. And no talking."

Naheed decided to sit down right where she was.

It was okay. She'd see Eliza later at lunch. Sitting with someone in the cafeteria was more of a statement anyway.

Just a snow day in September, Naheed told herself again.

The principal was standing at the front of the room, and one of the custodians was wheeling a podium across the floor. The teachers were still telling everyone to be quiet while the microphone was set up, and a loud screech from the amplifiers pierced the room. The principal began.

"I am sure you are all wondering why we are having

this unexpected assembly today. This is an unprecedented event, so there is really no, well, precedent for this. I mean to say, it is up to every school district to decide for themselves how to handle the events that have occurred."

There was the normal pushing and whispering and not paying attention.

"But as I have always believed in treating you students with respect, it is my policy that you should be informed. I also believe that incorrect information can lead to rumor and panic. But before I go on, I will first tell you we have decided not to close schools today. The rest of the day will proceed on a regular schedule. I repeat, we will follow a regular school schedule, and dismissal will be routine. However, all after-school activities have been canceled."

The noise in the room lessened. Naheed could feel her chest tighten. Maybe this wasn't a snow day, or a free day, or a broken septic system like the one that had closed school for a whole week last year.

Something was definitely wrong.

"There have been three attacks on the United States this morning."

Movements and the rustle of clothing, the tapping of feet, the ambient whispering, suddenly stopped.

"One in New York City at the World Trade Center. One in Washington, DC, on the Pentagon. And another somewhere in rural Pennsylvania. We are safe here."

There suddenly wasn't enough air in the library for everyone to breathe. Naheed could feel it. She could see the principal talking and hear what he was saying, but nothing was making sense. It was like he was an actor in one of those end-of-the-world movies. This wasn't real.

"There is nothing to be afraid of. Some parents have called the school and are on their way to pick up their children. If your parent is one of those, you will be notified in your classroom. Again, you will go to your regular fifth-period class. Thank you, and now your teachers will direct everyone back to their classrooms. And there will be no more discussions about this until further notice."

As soon as the principal walked away from the podium, the noise level in the room rose, like a boiling kettle that suddenly started to steam. Everyone began talking. A few girls started crying, like those few girls will always do.

Now Naheed knew for sure what Eliza had been upset about in science and why Mrs. Salinger had snapped off the television. Why parents were running to school to pick up their kids. But still it felt far away. There were things like this on the news all the time, weren't there? Bad things, scary things.

Life wasn't a movie.

It was going to be okay.

Wasn't it?

Naheed slowly stood with the rest of her class, uncertain of what she had just been told, voices rising up around her.

"My grandmother lives in Pennsylvania."

"An attack? What does that mean?"

"My dad lives in New York."

"They probably went after all those secrets stored in the Pentagon. I bet they stole all our secret files and spies and stuff."

"No, I heard it was a bomb."

"It's not a bomb. If it was a bomb, we'd all be in those underground shelter places."

"It's no big deal. It's not like it's a war or anything. They always want to scare us with this stuff."

And so on.

The students started to shuffle back to their classrooms. The gym teacher let Naheed's class have a study hall, but no one was allowed to even whisper. Naheed took out her math work and tried to concentrate, but by the end of the day many kids had gone home, and with each one leaving, another little bit of information from the outside world got left behind.

Hijackers.
The World Trade Center.
Fire.

When the bell rang for dismissal, the remaining students all poured out to the front of the school, and with no teachers to stop them, everyone was talking. The buses sat idling with their doors wide open.

People jumping to their deaths.
Plane crashes.
The White House evacuated.

When was this end-of-the-world movie going to be over?

There was Eliza standing in line, waiting to step up onto her bus, and Naheed's plan for apologizing to her seemed a hundred years in the past. It seemed like a silly speck of sand in a sandbox that was getting bigger and bigger with every frightful story that flew from parent to kid, from brother to sister, from friend to friend, from one kid to another.

Air travel grounded.

Buildings collapsing.

All at once Naheed knew she needed to get home. She hurried along the sidewalk and found her own bus, number fifteen.

"I heard it was terrorists," the boy in the front of the line was saying. He sounded almost excited.

Naheed couldn't see whom he was talking to. She could hardly hear above the sound of her own heart pounding.

"What do you mean, *terrorists*?" someone else asked.

Naheed could hear her own exaggerated breathing inside her head like she was inside a wind tunnel. People were starting to push, to stand as close to one another as they could, backpacks bumping, everyone's feet taking little steps closer to the doors. Naheed felt the heat of the sun warming her hijab. She brushed away a band of sweat that formed on her brow. She tried to calm herself.

Three more steps and Naheed would be on the bus, that much closer to home. Just breathe.

Two more steps.

She'd find a seat. Everything was going to be okay.

"It was Arabs." The voice rose above the others.

One more step.

"Yeah, you know, Muslims. The ones with those things on their heads."

Naheed didn't get on the bus.

It was just after three. The sky was clear, quiet, and the bluest blue she had ever seen. Naheed stepped out of line. She hiked her backpack up over her shoulder and took off down the access road toward the elementary school. Their school got out an hour after the middle school. It was about a half-mile walk. She needed to find her sister.

One Year Later

September 11, 2002
Ground Zero, New York City

At first it had been exciting, like being famous. Certainly, it was as close to being famous as pretty much anyone from Shanksville had ever been. There were news vans set up like permanent trailer parks—surrounding the strip mine, outside the school, and along US Route 30. There were satellite dishes and food trucks and newspeople everywhere. There were people who just felt they had to come, to see the site of such a tragedy and pay some kind of respect to those who had died.

There were the others: the conspiracy theorists, the morbidly curious, the wannabes, and the just plain crazy.

And then there were the families and friends of the victims of 9/11 and Flight 93, who came almost immediately after the crash, whose swollen eyes were ringed with black circles, whose hearts were cracked open and torn apart. They had come looking for an answer or a story or a piece of something, anything, to take away with them.

But there was nothing.

No answers. No closure. Nothing to take away.

So instead they *left* something.

They left stuffed animals, notes, ribbons, pieces of clothing, books, flowers, Bibles, flattened pennies, poems, photographs, jewelry, tiny trinkets. They tied their objects, their hearts, their sorrow, to the forty-foot-long chain-link fence that had been installed at the crash site; they wrote things on the tall white boards that had been put up for that purpose.

All kinds of people, hundreds a day, driving down roads that, a year ago, only a few cars and a couple of kids on their bicycles had traveled.

For a while Will's sisters set up camp on their front lawn just to give directions to all the visitors who inevitably made a wrong turn or two. They dragged out a folding table and chair and hung a sign: FREE DIRECTIONS. They took turns sitting there for weeks, until the grass under their chair turned brown, until even they got overwhelmed by all the people, the endless stream of lost, brokenhearted, patriotic, curious people. So much pain it wore a path in the streets and across everyone's hearts, threatening to obliterate everything else.

And this, the one-year anniversary, only promised to bring more interlopers. It was an opportune time, Will's mother had decided, for the family to get out of town, far from Somerset County, away from the crowds that had taken over Shanksville.

And where else to escape the crowds?

To New York City.

Seriously?

But Will knew why his mother had wanted to come. She had been awarded tickets to the 9/11 memorial service for her charity work, because she had spent the better part of the entire last year helping to set up the temporary memorial. She was in charge of cataloging every single item that was left behind or mailed to Shanksville. No object was too small or invaluable for her attention, not a water-soaked matchbook, not a box of broken crayons, not an empty wallet with barely visible initials stamped into one corner.

With each recorded memento of grief, Will's mother found hope and Will's family began to heal. The heroes of Flight 93 affected Will's family in a different way than they might have affected someone else's family. The people in that plane were heroes in the most important way—making a choice, not knowing the outcome, but knowing that acting was better than not acting. Doing the right thing because the right thing was what you were supposed to do. Only this time the whole country was mourning with Will's family.

Rooney and Callie just seemed excited to be in New York City. They all had taken the train yesterday from Johnstown to Penn Station and found their room at the Milford Hotel, right in Times Square.

The entire day they had acted like regular tourists. They walked four across along Broadway, craning their necks, looking up at the giant billboards and down at the rows of window displays, cameras, suitcases, NYC memorabilia, clothing stores, makeup stores. On Fifth Avenue there were entire stores devoted to just one designer, to sunglasses, to Nike, to the NBA, which of course Will wanted to go to and his sisters didn't complain too much about.

If this was the only part of New York City a person came to, he might never know any different. The city was alive with shopping and sightseeing, smells of steaming hot dogs and salty pretzels on every block. Vendors selling hats, selling pocketbooks, selling photographs.

"Look, Mom." Callie stopped and pointed.

A man sat on a tiny folding stool before a trifold display of photographs, mostly of the New York skyline.

"These photos will be worth a fortune one day," the man took the opportunity to say. "Photos of the World Trade Center. I took them myself."

Will scrunched up his face. It didn't seem likely. He had seen the exact same photo at another guy's booth a block away.

"No, thank you," Will's mother said.

This morning, Wednesday, September 11, they had to be downtown by eight o'clock. The reading of the names would begin at the exact time that the first plane had struck the first tower, 8:46. There were sure to be crowds. They were sure to have trouble with the subway map. They were sure to get lost at least once, so they left the hotel at seven in the morning and arrived at Ground Zero in plenty of time.

Some people will say that the distance a person happened to be from where one of the planes went down is in direct proportion to how deeply they were affected by the events of a day that came to be called simply 9/11. For instance, people who lived in Lower Manhattan were more a part of the tragedy than those who happened to be on the Upper West Side, than those who lived in Westchester County, or who were in school in upstate New York, or who called Seattle, Washington, home.

But that isn't true.

And some people point to the number of deaths—more than 2,700 at the World Trade Center, 343 of them firefighters, 246 in four planes, 125 in the Pentagon, citizens from over ninety different countries—but that doesn't quite tell the story either.

Because in the end it was just about people: mothers, fathers, friends, foes, sisters, brothers, children born and not yet born, sons and daughters; people from all over the United States and then all over the globe, whose lives would never be the same. Because the world changed that day, slowly and then all at once.

There were stories, so many stories. They started appearing immediately, everywhere in New York; stapled, taped, thumbtacked all over the city, photographs and photocopies, flyers, letters, sticky notes, and desperate pleas.

Please. Please, have you seen this woman, this man?

In the aftermath of the fallen towers thousands of people were missing. *Thousands.* The city became a giant scrapbook, a living, breathing, weeping album of the missing; every telephone pole, the side of every building, every tree, had become a collage of faces, an entreaty to understand, to share, and to find answers and mourn.

Aimee's mother hadn't been able to get a flight home to Los Angeles until that Friday, and when she did, she said it was like entering a military zone. At JFK Airport army personnel were everywhere. No one in line spoke above a whisper. Scheduled flights were delayed by hours, security took an unprecedented length of time, the flight itself was terrifying, but on Saturday morning when Aimee woke up, her mother was standing in her bedroom doorway.

And a year later they had decided they all had to return, together, for the one-year anniversary.

Sergio would be there, of course. Gideon had gotten him an extra ticket from the guys at Engine 209, Ladder Company 10, to attend the ceremony at Ground Zero inside the roped-off area, right on the flat expanse of dirt where the Twin Towers once stood. Sergio needed to be there. He wanted to. So much had happened in a year.

It wasn't going to be a holiday, not like Presidents' Day or MLK Day, so there was still school that Wednesday, but it was called Patriot Day and he was given permission to miss school.

His grandmother wanted to go with him, and they both stood for nearly an hour before they could even get in. Apparently, a lady was going to play the flute and, one after another, relatives of those who were killed were going to walk up onto the stage and read the names, nearly three thousand, out loud. Many of Gideon's friends were among them. Gideon himself was going to be one of the readers.

This last year Sergio had spent a lot of time at the firehouse, and Gideon had even come to visit them in Red Hook. Sergio's grandmother made dinner, and the three of them stuffed themselves, and they watched *Jeopardy!* on television afterward.

Gideon helped Sergio with his homework, not that Sergio needed it. Gideon taught him basic first aid, and when Sergio had a test in biology, they studied together. And in a funny way, having Gideon in his life, and knowing what had happened to the country, made Sergio less angry at his father, less angry at the world. It had made him more afraid and less afraid, both. There was so much to mourn, and so much to be proud of, so many reasons to be at this memorial.

Naheed and her family were making the pilgrimage as well, all the way from Columbus, Ohio, even though there had been days this past year when they had been afraid to leave their house.

That afternoon, a year earlier, Naheed and her sister had walked home together—nearly two full miles. Uncle Iman and Aunt Judith were still there and wouldn't be able to leave for weeks. Naheed's father was pulling into the driveway. Her mother had also left work early. She rushed into the house, with tears in her eyes. She pulled her daughters close and held them there.

"So many people," she kept saying. "So many people."

She had the look on her face, of a pain that was not her own but was for the whole world, that look that most all grown-ups seemed to express in those following days. Naheed and Nouri listened to and watched the television, but it all seemed too horrible to be real and too far away to have any significant impact on them personally.

Until a brick came sailing through the air a few weeks later, breaking glass and landing on their living-room floor.

Until a Middle Eastern restaurant in Columbus was targeted by a firebomb. "It's owned by Israelis, for heaven's sake," Naheed's father kept saying.

Until a gas station attendant in New Jersey was shot, not a Muslim, but a Sikh from India, because he was wearing his traditional turban.

And now Naheed's parents were taking them to New York, right into the belly of the beast, to grieve with the rest of the country, because her father vowed, "We are Americans, and no one is going to take that away from us."

For so many complicated reasons there would never be another morning as simply beautiful as September 11, 2001. People always talk about the weather when they don't have anything else to talk about, when the conversation is light, or feels stilted, or someone is just too peaceful, lazy, or preoccupied to think about anything more taxing.

But after that day the weather, and the way people remembered it, became something more; something potentially more deceptive, and yet something much more meaningful, more fragile and rare, and even more beautiful.

Wednesday, September 11, 2002, was sunny but not as clear, and the wind blew unrelentingly across Manhattan.

Aimee held tight to her mother's hand as they moved through the crowds. Her father walked close behind them. They finally found a spot and stood for a while on the platform on Fulton Street, with the other people who had also stopped walking, who had also come to be part of something larger than they were, something that drew them to this place even though they knew no one personally who had vanished into the white-clouded air that day. They couldn't get any closer without a ticket, and the streets were roped off for blocks.

Below, at the memorial, they could see those who were standing, the families of the victims, holding flags, clutching flowers, holding photographs, holding babies in the air, as if those looking down, and those far above, could see them and know and feel.

"It could have been you, Mom," Aimee whispered, because how many times had she wondered why and why not? Who gets a second chance? A third? A fourth? And why did someone else get none?

It had taken Aimee a while to find the kind of girls that she felt comfortable with in her new school, and it wasn't that Bridget and Vanessa were enemies or anything, but Aimee didn't need that kind of drama. Not after what she had been through.

"I want to go down there," Aimee said.

The warm air blew persistently, as if trying to drive away the sunshine. Above, the flags snapped like whips, and the crooning of the wind harmonized with the steady sound of human crying.

"That's just for family," her father said.

"I know, but I just need to stand there, or get a little closer at least. For one second." For a full year Aimee hadn't wanted to let her mother out of her sight. She had nightmares and got stomachaches when her mother went away on trips. But now Aimee let go of her mother's hand and headed toward the line of people inside the velvet ropes. Her mother reached out to stop her.

"Let her go," her father said. "We'll wait right here. Aimee," he called out. "We'll be right here. Don't be long."

She turned back around once and nodded. She needed to let go and she needed to grab on, and she needed to stand directly in the center of the universe that almost wasn't.

"We don't have to stay long, but I want to be there. I just want to leave these there. I need to show the world that we are Americans too. We can't be afraid," Naheed's mother said. She was clutching a spray of orchids wrapped in clear cellophane. "There's a fence surrounding the platform. We can't get too close, but I know we can get there and leave these flowers."

But Naheed *was* afraid. She understood what her parents were telling her, but she didn't see why they had to come all the way to New York City to show it. In many ways she felt like she was constantly saying "I'm sorry" for something she didn't do. Naheed and her family had as much in common with Islamic extremists as, well, nothing.

There was nothing about her religion that was like that of the terrorists who had done this, but no one really seemed to understand that. There had been community rallies and outcries against the violence, but that hadn't changed anything. Wearing her hijab, which had once seemed an ordinary act, even if it sometimes got her unwanted attention, was now nothing less than a unifying act of faith and bravery.

Naheed had worn her hijab to school the very next day. "I am proud of you," her father told her. "Courage is contagious: When one person of courage stands up, others are affected and stand up with him."

It was one thing to wear her religion on her sleeve, so to speak, at school, in the town where she had lived all of her life, with kind teachers and a principal to help explain things, but coming here, to New York, to Ground Zero?

That was a whole other kind of courage.

Yet Naheed couldn't help being moved by the sights around her, and she forgot what others might be thinking when they saw her. Their mother handed each of her daughters a stemmed blossom to slip into the chain-link fence. Naheed brought the flower to her face as she remembered that day, a year ago, when nothing else was important to her except fitting in, being like every-one else. Now when she looked around at the crowd of people, all sharing the same moment, the same sadness, not one person was like any other. If she squinted her eyes, everyone, every single person, melted into a mix of shapes and colors.

"What are you people doing here?"

A mix of shapes and colors, and a harsh, angry voice.

"Did you hear me? What are you people doing here?"

Was this voice talking to her? Naheed looked up.

He was white. He was big. He held an American flag in one hand. He stood directly in front of Naheed and her mother and sister, until her father stepped in front of his family.

Aimee heard it too. The angry voice. She couldn't get down to where the stage was set up, but she had made her way to the tall fence where people had hung photos and flowers and stuffed animals. Anger sends out a strange energy, like a force field in a science fiction movie. It repels.

It destroys.

Aimee felt it.

"I said, what are you people doing here?"

She turned to see whom the voice was talking to, where his hostility was directed, to whom.

"We are here to honor those who died, just like you are," a dark-skinned man answered. He spoke softly. He was with a woman and two girls, all three with those colorful veils on their heads.

"Well, we don't want your kind here. Nobody does. Get out and take your A-rab wife and kids with you."

It wasn't right. It wasn't fair. It was scary and it was racist. Will could hear the lady playing the flute and the names being read, slowly, one after the other in alphabetical order, behind him. But this was New York City, right? Nobody did anything for anyone else in New York City. People were rude and unfriendly here, even if he hadn't experienced any of that himself, except that the man at the information booth at Penn Station had been pretty gruff.

Somebody should do something.

It's not someone else's job. His father had taught him that.

It's all of our jobs.

This was just a family. Maybe they had lost someone. Maybe that's why they were here. To let go. To heal, like everyone else.

Will turned to see if his mother had heard it too, but it didn't look like she had. She was staring down at the proceedings and crying, not falling apart, but crying. The girls were on either side of her, holding her skirt.

Sergio noticed the father first, then he recognized the anger and the familiar sick feeling in the pit of his stomach. The anger was coming from the huge white man who was waving his flag around. The father wasn't going to fight, anyone could tell that. Anyone who had ever been in a fight could see that. He was leaning back, pressing his body against his wife and holding his arms behind him, creating a space where his family would be safe. He wasn't going to fight even if it came to that.

"We are not bothering anyone. We came here all the way from Ohio," the father said. "To pay our respects."

It wouldn't be much of a fight, anyway. The father looked to be about five six, maybe 150 pounds, and this white dude could have been Ivan Drago from *Rocky IV* without the accent.

* * *

Maybe the dad, who was there with his family, thought the other, bigger man would back away if he identified himself as being from Ohio; like Aimee was from California. *We are all Americans here.*

"We're from Ohio," the father said again. "I'm a physician."

But the other guy didn't seem to care and he didn't back away. He took another menacing step toward the family. Aimee looked back to see if her mother and father were watching. Could they see?

Was somebody going to help?

Was anybody going to do something?

And suddenly there were two boys, a white boy and a black boy, standing in front of the family; and then a whole bunch of firemen in their blue FDNY T-shirts seemed to come out of nowhere to stand next to the boys; and then a young mother, with her baby strapped to the front of her body, joined them; and then an old man and old woman in matching plaid shirts pinned with ribbons and buttons that said NEVER FORGET stood next to them; until there were so many people standing in front of the family that Aimee couldn't see them anymore.

All she could see was a sea of people, who could not

be more different but could not be more the same, standing together. And what she could hear, releasing into the air with the sounds of the flute, were the names of those who had died, in this very spot, remembered always, floating on the music of a warm September wind.

Author's Note

Like most everyone else over a certain age, I can remember exactly where I was when I first began hearing the news about the events of September 11, 2001. I had gone to the YMCA early that morning to swim laps, and on my way home I was listening to public radio out of New York City. The early report was that a small plane had accidentally crashed into one of the towers of the World Trade Center. I was driving down Route 7 in Wilton, Connecticut. I looked up at the sky. It was the clearest blue, with the calmest air, the most perfect temperature. I had just swum my seventy-two laps and I felt wonderful, while the voices on the radio were trying to make sense of how this could have happened. It's not like someone could just bump into the World Trade Center.

Maybe the pilot was ill. Maybe the small plane had lost control. They bantered about it my entire drive, about seven minutes.

My two boys, eleven and fourteen, were at school, but my husband was still home, about to leave for work. By the time I walked into the bedroom, where the TV news was on, a second plane—and they were now both identified as commercial airliners—had just crashed into the second tower. It became instantly, if not understandably, clear to everyone that this was intentional. My husband and I stood transfixed, as I imagine most of the country was, staring at the screen. We watched as the towers burst into flames. We watched when they began to fall. My husband didn't go to work that day. Everything shut down.

After that my memory is fuzzy. We live about an hour outside of New York City, and many of our friends, and parents of our children's friends, work in the financial district, where the World Trade Center once stood. My younger sister lived in the East Village of Manhattan. The son of my husband's college roommate lived in Brooklyn. My best friend's husband was scheduled for a meeting that morning in the Twin Towers themselves. And so on and so on.

After an assembly at my older son's high school,

during which the principal gave out just enough information to panic everyone, it was bedlam in the halls. Later we would hear stories. One Muslim girl in ninth grade, fearing for her safety, called her parents and asked to be picked up, but not before she was intimidated by angry comments. My son's baseball coach jumped into his car and made his way *toward* New York City to find his son. When the roads were blocked with fifty miles still to go, he got out and walked.

My younger son, who was in middle school, had been kept in the dark all day. They had been told only that something bad had happened in New York City. He didn't understand how bad until he saw me standing at the front door, anxiously waiting for him to get off the bus, my face streaked with tears. I could not stop crying.

In one beautiful clear-blue morning the whole world had suddenly changed. In the following days we walked around in shock, trying to figure out how to adjust, how to live in this new order of things. New words leaped into our vernacular, like "terrorism," "Homeland Security," "al-Qaeda," "Ground Zero." And they have remained.

For young students today there is no "before 9/11." I think that's why I wanted to write this story. When I was in school, I learned about historic events like the

Holocaust and Pearl Harbor as things that had happened in the past, long ago. And as much as I was aware that these terrible events had altered the global consciousness, I had never lived through one. I didn't know what that really meant. Now I had witnessed another seismic shift, when the world in which I was raising my children stood, for one long day, completely and horrifically still, and we all wondered how, or if, we were ever going to be the same again.

In order to magnify the division between "before 9/11" and "after 9/11," I chose to tell the story of four American children in just those forty-eight hours before each of their lives would be directly affected by the events of that day. I also made a choice that the characters in this story would not lose anyone that day, and although that might not be the most realistic way to encapsulate 9/11, it was something I felt I had to do. I chose the structure of this story to reflect a theme of interconnectivity in our society, in particular between children. I wanted to show how in the end this tragic, divisive event actually brought complete strangers together instead of tearing them apart, which is, I imagine, the ultimate goal of terrorism.

Acknowledgments

There are many people I need to acknowledge for their help in writing this book. For how the story evolved from the shape it was in at the beginning, I owe enormous gratitude to not only my editor—the intelligent, insightful, and meticulous Reka Simonsen—but to my agents, Marietta Zacker and Nancy Gallt.

Marietta had the unfortunate job of mucking through and addressing some very convoluted tangential plot lines and characterizations before Reka even saw my "first" (yeah, right) draft. I am deeply appreciative.

Reka, who wouldn't let me off the hook for anything and who guided me to continue searching until I could truly speak for these four brave children—I cannot thank you enough.

To Erica Stahler, copyeditor extraordinaire, thank you for your amazing work at figuring out complicated time lines and geography, and for enforcing accuracy in order to honor a truth and a tragedy.

To Erin McGuire and Russell Gordon, thank you for the beautiful jacket, which I hope speaks for itself with its simplicity and depth, but personally, I was blown away by it.

To Stasha Gibb, the wonderful librarian at the McDonogh School in Owings Mills, Maryland, who is now a friend, for her help with the Muslim cultural details. I battered her with questions and then made her read the whole manuscript in its early form—thank you, Stasha.

To my dear friend, Homa Sadeghian, MD, who patiently supplied me with just the right Persian expressions. Thank you. Thank you to Reno Barkman, present-day principal of the Shanksville-Stonycreek middle and high schools. With suspicion at first (and why not? Shanksville is still the target of gawkers) and then incredible generosity, Mr. Barkman talked to me on the phone at length. He also put me in touch with two young men who were middle school students in Shanksville in 2001. Thank you, Jacob Miller and Jeffrey T. Berkey. You painted a picture for me of life in a very small town, turned upside down. Mr. Barkman also put me in touch with the truly heroic Connie Hummel, the principal in Shanksville on September 11, 2001. Her story deserves its own book.

Thank you to my old friend Wendy Mass, for giving me permission to write this ambitious story and then giving me the title, right there on the spot.

Thank you to my dear friend Elise Broach, who supports me in life and in writing, in more ways than she knows.

Thank you to all my friends who listened to me hash out this story and shared with me all their experiences from that day, including Susan, Batya, Jill, Dal, Gail, and my sons, Sam and Ben.

And thank you, thank you, thank you to Steve, for allowing me this wonderful life I lead. And for loving me.

A Reading Group Guide for
Nine, Ten: A September 11 Story
by Nora Raleigh Baskin

Discussion Questions

1. Talk about the book's title, prologue, and structure, including the book's division into days and the headings at the beginning of each chapter. Why did the author choose to emphasize dates and times? How does the prologue create tension and foreshadowing?
2. Why do you think the author opened the first chapter in an airport? Why is each of the four protagonists at O'Hare? What small connections occur between them at the airport?
3. At the end of the first chapter, what do you know about each protagonist and his or her family? Given what you know about 9/11, what predictions did you have about each main character and what would happen to him or her in the rest of the story? What led you to those predictions? Did they come true by the end of the book?
4. Why did the author choose to portray protagonists from all over the country? How are the four of them similar? In what important ways are they different?

5. Discuss the struggles in Will's life from his father's death. What are his feelings about his father's last actions? How does 9/11, and especially the flight that crashed near Will's hometown, change his feelings?
6. What roles do the other fathers, or their absences, play in the story? Compare and contrast the fathers, what they do, and how they act.
7. Similarly, what roles do mothers, or their absences, play? Compare and contrast the mothers, what they do, and how they act. Include Sergio's grandmother in the discussion.
8. How is Aimee's life in flux even before the terrorist attacks? What are her feelings about the move and her mother's job? What are her concerns about her parents? How does her mother's job and trip to New York increase tension for the reader?
9. Sergio makes a strong connection with a firefighter named Gideon. Describe how they meet and what motivates them to become friends. How does knowing Gideon change Sergio's response to 9/11? Why is Gideon important in Sergio's life a year later?
10. What is a hijab and why does Naheed wear one? She describes the first time she wore one as being enveloped "in tradition and love." What does she mean?

What problems does it cause her? Discuss why others sometimes react negatively or nervously to her.

11. Discuss Naheed's family and their religious beliefs. In what ways do her parents and her uncle disagree? What are their different ideas about what Naheed's life should be like? Naheed and her sister react differently from each other when confronted with questions about their religion. What are the differences, and what explains them?
12. Analyze Naheed's relationship with Emily and what causes Naheed to be mean to the other girl. How does Naheed feel afterward, and how does she plan to make it up to Emily? Why do you think the author included this conflict as part of the plot?
13. Both Naheed and Sergio think about becoming doctors when they grow up. Why is each of them interested in being a doctor? In what ways is that dream different for each of them because of their life circumstances?
14. What are some of the similarities in what the protagonists do on September 10? What are some common threads in their lives on that day? What are the significant differences?
15. How do the terrorist attacks and the crash of Flight 93 change life in Shanksville? How do they affect

Will's mother? What draws different visitors to the town, and what do they do there?

16. The final chapter takes place on September 11, 2002. Using details in the chapter, talk about how life has changed for each of the protagonists because of the terrorist attacks. How does each of them end up at the memorial service?
17. Naheed's father states, "We are Americans, and no one is going to take that away from us." What leads him to declare that? Why does the angry flag-holding man in the last chapter yell at Naheed's family? How do others defend them, and why?
18. The author's note gives readers insight into her experiences on September 11. Discuss her description of the day and draw connections between it and the novel. How does she show in the novel that 9/11 brought strangers together?